My Heritage

AGU, JAACHYNMA N.E.

My Heritage

ISBN: 9785033716
ISBN-13: 978 -978-50337-17

Published *by* Chiysonovelty International

Printed in the United States of America

CONTENTS

DEDICATION

To My
Goodly and Godly Heritages:
Aham, King and Edwald.

INTRODUCTION

You are born a royalty, you are God's offspring, you hail from Him, your origin is of Him and He is your place of nativity. Did this statement strike a chord within you? Did it awaken the sleeping giant inside of you? Then this book is for you!

No child of God is born sick, a weakling, a commoner or a pauper. The Bible describes Christ as the King of kings and Lord of lords; this simply means that Christ is the King over all kings and Lord over all lords. It further implies that we are kings and lords after His order.

Kings rule and dominate; they are not beggarly. Lords reign and take charge; they do not take orders from others. You are a king and a lord! Do not give that situation the privilege to rule over you. Do not give that challenge the authority to ride you. Wake up, shake yourself and take your position at the centre of events! Do not watch things happen around you, be the happening person in your world! This is your inheritance in Christ; yes, you have a goodly HERITAGE!

CHAPTER ONE

HEALING

Martins became an orphan at the tender age of five. Ruthless gunmen stormed their home one evening and killed his parents without mercy.

His father, Mr. Gregory, had been a staff of a multinational pharmaceutical firm. As a trained accountant, he headed the finance department of the firm. He was a handsome man, bold and courageous. He feared no one and treated everyone fairly. Martins was very proud of his dad, especially for his resoluteness in handling issues. Mrs. Gregory was an exciting woman, a homemaker. She was a trained staff nurse and midwife but her husband preferred her staying at home to take care of him and their kids to running shifts in a hospital. Martins was very close to his mother. They played and sang rhymes together. Martins had an elder sister, Irene, who was two years older than he was. Theirs was such a nice happy family.

When he lost both parents the same evening, something died in him and for a long while, the part of him that housed feelings remained locked with its key thrown away.

Martins became a defiant little brat; he hated everyone around him with a passion. After the burial of his parents, his dad's twin brother, Uncle Marc, took Martins and his sister to live with him.

Marc had married two women in a row and none of them gave him children. He treated his niece and nephew as his own children and cared for them in no little way.

Despite the love Uncle Marc showered on Martins and Irene, Martins remained unruly and moody to a fault. One hardly caught him smiling or joking. He always wore a hard, cold look. He became a source of concern to his sister as well as his uncle and aunt.

When he was ten years old, he went up to Uncle Marc and told him he wanted to leave the country. He was no longer interested in living in his country of nativity. Uncle Marc pleaded with him to reconsider his stand as he was still too young to travel to a foreign country unaccompanied. After much persuasion from his sister and Uncle Marc, he agreed to stay back. But his attitude became worse.

In school, though very brilliant, he hardly stayed in class. He bullied other kids and was very disrespectful to his teachers. The school authorities got tired of punishing him and finally expelled him. He left school and became worse in his infamy.

****

Sometime later, a relative of Rose, Uncle Marc's wife, came to the house. She was a young girl of about sixteen years of age. She was Irene's age mate. Martins, to everyone's surprise, warmed up to the girl. He chatted and played with her often.

Alicia was a warm, receptive and intelligent girl. She had guts that amazed all and she was witty as well. Alicia had lost her mother at birth and her father had married another woman who maltreated Alicia no end. She endured all the harsh treatments as she wasn't ready to allow her circumstances dominate her. She believed she was in this world for a purpose and that purpose she must fulfill come what may.

However, her maternal relatives weren't pleased with the treatment meted out to her so they requested her mother's immediate younger sister, Rose, to take her in since she and Marc had no children of their own. In this way, she came to live in the same house with Martins and Irene.

The moment Martins saw Alicia, he knew she had come for him. He warmed up to her effortlessly and before too long Martins began seeing things from a better perspective, though his attitude remained unimpressive.

One day, Alicia and Martins were home alone. Uncle Marc and Aunty Rose had gone to work and Irene had gone to school. Alicia was yet to start school because the current academic session had a few more weeks to end before a new one could begin. She was to be enrolled the following academic session. Of course, Martins wasn't in school anymore.

'Why aren't you in school?' Alicia asked Martins.

'I don't know,' was his curt reply.

'You don't know what?' Alicia asked.

Martins looked up from the scribbles he was making with a black pen, stared hard at her for what seemed like eternity, and went back to what he was doing.

'Young man, I asked you a question!' Alicia spoke so softly that Martins' heart ached.

'And I have answered you, young lady,' he replied.

'Tell you what?' Alicia began. 'Your life isn't going to turn out good if you continue this way. Yes, you lost your parents all in one day and you want to go on mourning them for life. Have you asked yourself what your parents' feelings and reactions will be if they see what you are doing to yourself and to the people around you? The only way you show dead loved ones that you cared for them and loved them is by continuing the projects and legacies they left behind. But, if you throw their ideals and legacies to the wind, it means you never loved them. I put it to you, Martins, that you don't have an iota of love for your late parents. You are simply a selfish, silly brat!' she spat out and dashed out of the room.

'What just happened? What did she just say?' Martins asked no one in particular.

Is she in any way referring to me? Who does she think she is? Maybe she hasn't been told my story, that I'm as hard as diamond and as cold as ice. She is yet to learn that none penetrates me, he thought as he made his hand into a fist and hit it hard on the bedside table. He picked up the pen he had been holding earlier, dropped it again in frustration and lay back on his bed, staring at the ceiling.

The whole drama between them replayed itself a few times in his head, and the last time it wasn't Alicia's voice he heard but his late mom's voice. He jumped off the bed, opened his door and peered outside, but seeing no one in sight, he stepped back into his room. He began pacing the floor as the voice kept reverberating in his mind.

'You never loved them . . . you don't have an iota of love for your late parents!' the voice kept repeating, getting harsher each time. When he couldn't bear it any more, he sat down on the floor and began to weep. He wept himself sore and slept off without knowing when. He dreamt of his mother. She was asking him why he was being very unfair to the people that love him so much. She told him that Irene, though older than him, was left under his care as a man but he had chosen to fail everybody and dash the hope of sweet Irene. She told him they were not impressed at all with his attitude. He woke up from that dream terrified out of his wits, for he had never seen his mom that furious in real life.

He sat on his bed, held his head in his hands for a while before tears began rolling down his cheeks. He cried uncontrollably for a long time and then made a resolve. He stood up from his sitting position, moved towards the door, as he reached out for the knob, the door flew open and Irene walked in. She stared at him and burst into tears.

'Hey, what's the matter?' he asked, not knowing whether to go and hold her or to let her cry her misery away. She didn't respond but continued sobbing.

Martins was getting more confused by the second. 'What's the meaning of all these?' he wondered. Impulsively, he approached his sister, touched her gently on the shoulders, but she didn't bulge. He went closer and placed his two arms around her. She leaned her head on his shoulder and wept the more.

Though two years his senior, Irene looked frail and fragile so that many people thought Martins was older. He held his sister while she sobbed. After a while she quietened down, dried her eyes walked towards the door. As she got to the door, she glanced back, muttered 'thank you' and left as unceremoniously as she entered.

Martins was too confused to think straight. Everything that had happened since morning was too strange for his comprehension. Were these accidents or incidents? He stood there a little longer and went back to sit at his reading table, took a pen and brought out a writing pad. He toyed with them awhile and began to write. Tears soiled the first sheet of paper he wrote on. He tore it off the notepad, squeezed it and threw it into the wastepaper basket beside his chair. He started writing again; he wrote five letters in all and addressed them to different folks in his life. He sat back to read the one he addressed to himself, it read thus:

Martins,

Sit up and live out the dreams your father had for you. Wipe the tears of your mother and only sibling, Irene. Don't cause

Irene and Uncle Marc any more pains. You are in this world for a purpose, search it out and fulfill it. Go back to your studies, don't let the desires of those wicked people who murdered your parents come to fruition. Never give them the chance to laugh heartily; if you continue on that wrong track, you are giving them cause to gloat triumphantly over you and what remains of your family. It is often said and believed that hurting people hurt others. Martins, don't live out this cliché. Change, and do so now!

Frankly yours,

Martins.

As he read the letter to himself, he made a firm resolve to succeed despite all odds.

He went to Uncle Marc and Aunty Rose later that evening, handed them a copy of the letter he wrote and apologised genuinely for his childish and selfish behaviour. He begged them to enrol him in another school so he could continue with his studies. His uncle and aunt were so happy and quickly obliged his request.

Martins started school again and his performance was great. He had a competitor in his class, a girl named Jina. Initially he wanted to be at war with her but decided to be friends with her instead. They became inseparable to the amazement of everybody. They were nicknamed 'Mr. and Mrs.' by their classmates. He was about sixteen months older than Jina, but they had respect for each other. During their final year, Martins did so well that he won a scholarship to further his studies abroad. He was elated at the news, but felt bad when he learnt Jina didn't get the same opportunity. He wondered how he was going to cope without Jina. They were so close to each other.

Jina couldn't go with him even if she wanted to because her mother was poor and only worked as a maid for a wealthy family who had little or no regards for Jina and her mom. Secondly, Jina was asthmatic and allergic to cold regions. And Canada, where he was going to, was quite cold.

As the day of his departure drew near, his pains increased. He didn't want to go without Jina, yet he couldn't go with her.

Jina and her mother came to their house on the eve of his departure to bid him farewell. Amidst tears he promised to always write her and never lose touch with her. Jina had gotten admission into Abbas University situated in the same city where they lived.

For the umpteenth time, Martins wished Jina was travelling with him. As Jina and her mother made to leave, Martins removed his shirt and placed it on Jina's shoulders, covering her with it.

She looked at him in bewilderment and asked, gesturing at the shirt on her shoulders, 'Martins, what are you doing? What am I supposed to do with this?'

'Hold it, cherish it and let it continually remind you of me and my warm thoughts,' Martins explained.

'Thank you for being so thoughtful and inspiring,' Jina replied amidst tears. She removed the only bracelet she had and gave it to him. 'This is the only bracelet I have,' Jina said. 'But take it, make it your heritage,' she whispered sniffing harder in an attempt to stop the tears rolling down her cheeks.

'It is our heritage,' Martins whispered, holding her close to him as her tears stained his immaculate white T-shirt.

'Don't cry, Jina, everything will be all right, I believe,' Martins comforted, patting her back gently. Jina raised her head from his shoulder and looked into his eyes, her face tear-stained.

'Yes, I know that things will turn out very well for us, and soon too,' he reassured her.

Jina clung to him tightly, not wanting to let go for fear of losing him forever.

'My tender shoot, I will come back to you soon. Please be strong for me,' he begged.

Mrs. Jordan, who escorted her daughter to bid Martins farewell, watched the duo for a while and knew she had to stop them otherwise they would stay there forever. She cleared her throat gently but they were too engaged in their own world to notice. She did it again, this time louder. They disengaged but still held on to each other's hand.

'It's about time we leave for home, Jina,' she said. Turning to Martins, she said, 'Can we have a word of prayer, please?'

'With all pleasure, Ma,' Martins said, giving Jina's hand a squeeze before letting her go.

'Can we join our hands together?' Mrs. Jordan asked.

In response to the question they all moved closer to each other, joined their hands together and formed a little circle. They prayed for journeying mercies and guidance. Mrs. Jordan led the prayers. When they had shared the grace, they hugged one another lightly before dispersing.

Martins walked them to the gate holding Jina's hand and intermittently giving it a gentle squeeze. At the gate, they hugged, cried and reluctantly parted. Martins stood there watching them until they were out of sight. Then he turned around with hands in his pockets and strolled pensively back to the house.

****

Having cried so much the previous evening, Jina's health began to fail. She had a severe asthmatic attack in the early hours of that morning. There was no money to take her to the hospital, so her mother could only pray to God for the healing of her daughter. She prayed and reminded Jina of the divine healing and health that was part of the believer's heritage in Christ

Jesus. 'Healing is the children's bread,' she kept muttering to her daughter. 'By His stripes we were healed. Yes, He bore our infirmities and the chastisement of our peace was upon Him. Jina, you have been healed and you remain the healed of the Lord!' she kept declaring to Jina.

Jina could only nod her head in agreement as she whizzed. She closed her eyes so as not to see the agony etched on her mother's face. She prayed silently in her heart that the Lord would heal her and make her mother happy once more.

They were still in that prayer and pensive mood when they heard a loud knock on their door. Her mother stood to open the door. Scarcely had she reached the door when it flew open and in walked Mrs. Wilson, her boss.

'Good morning, Mrs. Wilson,' her mother greeted, stepping away from the door to allow the visitor in.

'What is good about this lousy morning, and why aren't you in the kitchen yet?' Mrs. Wilson spat out.

'I'm sorry, Ma'am. Jina isn't feeling too well,' Mrs. Jordan replied, gesturing towards Jina in bed.

'Oh! Really? I pay you and put a roof over your head! You should at least abide by my terms or get kicked out before you know it!' She snorted.

'I'm sorry, Ma'am,' Mrs. Jordan said. 'I was in the kitchen earlier this morning to fix the breakfast before coming here to attend to Jina,' she explained.

'Shut that dirty trap you call mouth. You don't decide when your chores are done. I call the shots here,' Mrs. Wilson roared. 'Now, get going,' she hissed.

Mrs. Jordan took one more tearful look at her daughter. Jina nodded briefly, indicating that she should go on to her duty post. Mrs. Jordan returned the nod, reassured that her daughter would be fine.

Mrs. Wilson half-pushed, half-dragged Jina's mother out of the room. Jina felt hot tears sting her eyes. She wished that things were different for them.

Just then, the door flew open again and Mrs. Wilson walked back into the room.

'Stop all this pretence, it will not help you one bit,' she taunted. 'I know you are not sick but merely pretending. And if you are, you might as well die so your excuse of a mother will concentrate on her job.' She finished, hissed loudly and walked out of the room.

Jina thought she was going to die from the pain that hit her heart with those hateful words. She tried sitting up to face the woman who just spilt such venom from her bosom. As she did, she saw the inscription hanging behind the door, for Mrs. Wilson had left, shutting the door after her. The inscription had hung there for as long as Jina remembered, but it had never meant much to her. As she looked at it this time, the words seem so real and energetic: 'Look And Live!'

Under the write up was the picture of Moses lifting up the bronze serpent. Jina looked harder and saw that there were other writings on it. Why hadn't she noticed them all these years, she asked herself.

A tiny voice within her spoke, *'Because you haven't looked.'*

She looked around her in bewilderment to see who spoke to her, but she didn't see anyone.

'It must have been my imaginations,' she thought as she took her gaze back to the picture frame. Now the other writings on it appeared bolder, she could read them clearly from where she was: Numbers 21:8 (*MSG*), *'. . . whoever is bitten and looks at it will live.'*

'That sounds interesting,' she muttered to herself.

She peered again and saw another scripture from the New Testament written under the first one. It was from John 3: 14-15 (MSG) '. . . *Moses lifted the serpent in the desert so people could have something to see and believe, it is necessary for the Son of Man to be lifted up—and everyone who looks up to Him will gain a real life, eternal life.'*

Jina put her feet down on the floor as her heart thumped faster. This time there wasn't the usual asthmatic pains, but pure excitement. She had found the best and permanent cure for her ill health.

'*It's not your ill health,*' the tiny voice within her said again.

'Who are you?' Jina asked, puzzled about this voice that read her thoughts and responded to them.

'*I am your Friend, Teacher, Counsellor and Strengthener,*' the Voice replied, getting more audible as if excited at being recognized.

'My friend? I know all my friends' voices and I don't think yours sound like the voice of any of my friends,' she replied, looking around the room to see where a person might be hiding.

'You don't know Me but your mother does. She talks with Me and about Me always,' the Voice replied.

'What is your name?' Jina asked, flinging off the blanket her mother had used to cover her. Strange, she was sweating and feeling stronger by the second.

'Go to Acts 10:38 and read about Me,' the Voice replied.

'Are You the Lord? Oh my God!' Jina exclaimed, ecstatic.

Her mother often told her that the Lord was with them even during their worst situations. 'He comes to deliver us out of them all,' she recalled her mother saying to her time without number.

'*Get Acts 10:38,*' the Voice nudged Jina gently.

She took her mother's NIV Bible and searched the table of contents for the book of Acts. She quickly flipped to the chapter and verse and read out aloud, '*How God anointed Jesus of Nazareth with the Holy Spirit and power, and how he went around doing good and healing all who were under the power of the devil, because God was with him.'*

'Hmmm . . .' Jina breathed, 'are you Jesus of Nazareth?' she asked.

'I am the Holy Spirit—the Ability at work in Jesus of Nazareth,' the Voice replied.

'Oh!' Jina gasped as she used her two hands to cover her mouth.

'Why are You here?' she queried for lack of what else to say.

'To bring to fulfilment God's plans for your life,' the Voice echoed in her head.

'God can't have plans for a poor asthmatic girl like me,' Jina replied angrily.

'You are not asthmatic, you are not poor, and God has plans, great plans for you,' said the Voice tenderly.

His gentility was soothing and warm. Jina was still trying to come to terms with the reality of what was happening to her. Was she dreaming, in a trance or in reality? she wondered.

'But I am asthmatic and poor,' she insisted, trying to convince not only the Voice but herself, for in actual fact she had not felt the usual pains in her respiratory track since this conversation started.

'The Father has healed you through the stripes Jesus received before His death on the cross at Calvary,' explained the Voice. 'All you need to do,' the Voice continued, 'is to accept the Healer and access your healing heritage in Him.'

Then the door opened and Mrs. Jordan hurried into the room to check on her daughter. She stopped in her tracks as she saw her sitting up in bed with the Bible in her hands and beads of perspiration on her forehead. This wasn't the sight she had expected would greet her.

'Jina,' she whispered softly, coming closer her to feel her temperature. 'Are you okay?' she quizzed.

'Yes, Mother, I am fine,' Jina replied, smiling at the expression on her mother's face.

'What happened?' her mother asked, getting more perplexed.

'I have been talking with Someone,' Jina replied, still smiling.

Mrs. Jordan looked around the room but didn't see anyone. She looked at the telephone that hung on the wall; the receiver was in place just as she had left it.

'Who?' she asked, getting alarmed.

'He said He is your friend and that you talk with Him and about Him all the time,' Jina said with such softness that her mother's bottled up concern was uncorked.

The woman came closer and sat next to her daughter, looking at her intently to check for signs of mental imbalance. Jina wasn't looking as sick and frail as she had looked a few hours before, yet she wasn't making sense with her talking. *'What has happened to her?'* her mother thought.

'Jina Jordan! Please don't play games with me,' she warned. 'Now, tell me what you have been up to!' She was not finding the whole drama funny.

Jina laughed, placed her head on her mother's shoulder and almost in a whisper asked, 'Mother, who is the Healer? Do tell me about Him, please. The Voice that spoke with me in your absence told me to accept the Healer and access my divine heritage,' she explained.

'The Voice?' Mrs. Jordan asked as tears of relief gathered in her eyes and threatened to spill. She blinked rapidly to stop them from flowing, for she didn't want to let her daughter down at this precious moment. It registered in her mind that the Lord had been with her daughter all along. Why didn't she think of it earlier? He had promised to be with His children always, to the end of the age. No wonder she felt so calm and at peace while working and taking orders from Mrs. Wilson. The Lord was with Jina, thereby taking the weight of anguish and worry off her shoulders.

'Thank You, Lord Jesus!,' she sniffed as she drew her daughter close to herself and gently ran her hand up and down her back. 'The Healer is our Lord Jesus Christ,' she whispered to her daughter. 'Now, tell me all that He told you,' she pressed.

Jina inhaled and exhaled freely without the whizzing sound and pain associated with such simple tasks before her encounter this morning. She could now breathe in and out freely. She tried this several times and realised she had been perfectly made whole from the asthma disease.

'The Healer healed me, Mother, even without my asking Him to do it,' she said joyfully.

'Yes, beloved, He answers us even before we call,' her mother replied happily too. 'And you know, healing is His children's bread.'

CHAPTER TWO

EXCELLENT LIFE

Jina's journey with the Holy Spirit thus began. She confided in Him in all things and at all times. She excelled in health and life in general because the Holy Spirit always showed her the right buttons to press. Jina became a high flyer because she had accessed and could always access the Wisdom of God.

Mrs. Wilson found it difficult to understand Jina. The once shy and sickly girl had blossomed into a beautiful and lively girl. She was always smiling and humming a tune to herself. *'What brought about this kind of change,'* Mrs. Wilson wondered. She vowed to get to the root of it all and crush it. *'Nobody who is poor and works as a housemaid has the right to be that joyful and elegant,'* she thought.

Her husband had insisted their only child, Alfreda, go to the same university with Jina. His reason was so that Jina could take care of Alfreda. As good and reasonable as that sounded, Mrs.

Wilson wasn't happy that her precious only child was in the same school with Jina, a commoner! To make matters worse, both girls were in the same department and Jina was the brightest in their class.

On a number of occasions, their Head of Department had invited Mrs. Wilson to discuss Alfreda's nonchalant attitude towards her coursework and her lifestyle.

Mrs. Wilson hired some young guys in the school to monitor Jina and report all her dealings and moves to her. So far, they hadn't come up with any substantial information other than the fact that Jina withdrew to some quiet place all by herself to pray and read the Bible.

'Pray?' Mrs. Wilson snorted. 'Pray?' she spat again as if it was an abomination. She sighed for the zillionth time since she got that report. Jina could pray the whole day for all she cared. After all, prayer had never helped anybody. If it had, Mrs. Jordan, who prayed like no other person she knew, wouldn't have remained a poor housemaid. The prayers would have saved her and given her better opportunities, she mused.

'Prayer my foot!' she hissed.

She tried pushing Jina out of her thoughts but couldn't. *I have to do something to stop this brat's excessive achievement*, Mrs. Wilson thought. But, what would she do? In recent times she had done virtually everything she could think of, yet none of them seemed to dampen the girl's spirit.

****

Academically, Jina was a top-notcher. Many admired her intelligence, a handful hated her guts, but none could ignore her.

'You truly amaze me these days,' Mrs. Jordan said to her daughter one day.

'Why, Mom?' Jina asked, smiling.

'You are so full of life, joy and excitement,' Mrs. Jordan replied.

'It's the Lord's doing.' Jina smiled. 'I feel this thing always bubbling within me. Even when I pretend to be angry or ignore it, it's still there,' she explained.

'Oh dear, don't stop it. It's the joy of the Lord, one of the fruits of the Holy Spirit,' her mother explained to her, brushing back the strands of hair that escaped from the knot Jina made of her hair.

'He told me that,' Jina said, smiling at her mother.

'Oh! Jina, I'm really so happy for you,' her mother said, hugging her.

A knock on their door startled them. They glanced at each other, their eyes questioning, was either of them expecting a visitor? Jina shook her head, indicating, she wasn't.

'I'll get it then,' Mrs. Jordan said and headed towards the door. The knock came again, this time a little louder.

'Hold on,' Mrs. Jordan called out as she took hold of the door handle. She gently opened the door and found the security man standing there holding an envelope.

'Good morning, Old Soldier,' Mrs. Jordan greeted the old man.

'Good morning, Ma'am,' the man replied, smiling. Each time he was referred to as an old soldier, he beamed with excitement. It reminded him of his days in the 54th Brigade, where he worked steadfastly to defend the unity of his country. He was always telling stories of his days in the army. And if anyone tried to gainsay his story, he would ask, 'did you fight in Burma? I fought in Burma.' He often delivered this statement with a fist thumping his chest.

'It's a beautiful morning, isn't it?' Mrs. Jordan asked.

'Yes, it is. It looks like one of those days in the army when we were allowed to laze around after a hard morning drill,' the old soldier replied.

Mrs. Jordan smiled gently, not wanting to encourage him with the army tale. It would infuriate Mrs. Wilson no end if she saw both of them chatting on a morning like this. Yet, Mrs. Jordan didn't want to appear rude by asking Old Soldier to leave.

'How's my beautiful Jina?' Old Soldier asked. 'This is for her,' he said, stretching out the envelope to Mrs. Jordan before she had the chance to answer about Jina.

'Oh, thank you. I will give it to her right away,' she said.

'The mail man brought it earlier this morning,' he explained.

'Thank you once more,' Mrs. Jordan said.

'Say me well to her,' Old Solider said, walking away. He had only gone a few steps when the door to the main building opened and Mrs. Wilson stepped out.

'Old Solider!' she barked.

'Good morning, Ma'am,' the man replied in his usual calm manner.

'What are you doing here, away from duty post?' she asked.

'I came to check on little Miss Jina to see how she is doing,' Old Solider lied. Mrs. Wilson had ordered that all mails addressed to Mrs. Jordan or her daughter were to be brought to her first.

'Is that what I employed you for, checking on some worthless girl and her mother?' Mrs. Wilson queried. Old Solider didn't respond. He merely walked away, humming a tune to himself. This infuriated his employer the more.

'Old Solider!' she called once again in anger.

'Yes, Ma'am,' Old Soldier replied.

'Didn't I see the postman talking with you this morning?' she asked.

'Yes, he stopped by to exchange pleasantries and then he left,' Old Solider replied over his shoulder. He continued on his way, still humming his war tune.

Mrs. Wilson turned livid with rage. The old man had a way of belittling her and she hated his guts. Yet she felt helpless against him. She sighed and walked back into her house without as much as a glance towards Mrs. Jordan's residence.

****

Inside, Jina tore the envelope open and her heart gladdened at the sight of Martins' cute cursive handwriting. The letter read:

My Cutie,

How are you doing? How is your health and studies? I'm sorry it took me this long to reply your last mail. I have been quite busy with my academics. Pardon me, please! Yes, busy, but not too busy to remember you are there—

praying for me and loving me tenderly.

You are a gift from God to me. Your last letter set me thinking. It sounded like my mother was speaking to me via those lines. I cannot tell you categorically that my first love for Christ has been rekindled but I'm working on it. Your words of love, prayer and encouragement are fanning its embers into flame—and I'm so grateful for that.

How is your mom? I hope her employers aren't stressing her so much. Extend my love and warmth to her. We have some months before we start our final exams and, God helping me, I'm not leaving any stone unturned.

I am planning a trip home after the exams. If it works out it means I will see you before too long so we can plan our lives together.

Remain your good self and don't forget we are each other's inheritance.

I love you—yes, I really do.

Blessings always!
Martins

Jina smiled all through the letter and shut her eyes after reading it. When she opened her eyes again, she exhaled and offered up a prayer for Martins, 'Dear Lord, Martins' love for You will grow; he will serve you. Yes, we will serve you together, in Jesus' Name, Amen.'

'How is he?' her mother asked interrupting, her thoughts.

'Oh, he is good, Mom, and he sends his love,' she replied, beaming with excitement. 'He might be home for the holidays,' she continued.

'Oh, that will be nice,' her mother replied.

'And did you tell him about your faith?' her mother asked, cleaning her hand with a hand towel.

'Yes, I did and he didn't get angry. Here is what he said.' She stood up and showed the letter to her mom.

'Oh, thank God!' Mrs. Jordan exclaimed, handing the letter back to her daughter. 'This is so touching,' she continued. 'We will pray more for him; his soul is vital to God.'

'Yes, Mom, we will,' Jina replied, smiling.

CHAPTER THREE

RIGHTEOUSNESS

Jina was done with her final exams. She hadn't heard from Martins in a while but she attributed it to preparations for his final exams. She wondered where their friendship would get to. He had said in his last letter to her a few months back that they would plan their lives together. Things were happening pretty fast to be mere coincidences. At twenty, she was too young to be thinking about marriage but the pull towards that direction was getting stronger by the day.

One afternoon she was alone in their apartment. Having thought a lot about her future and friendship with Martins, she began a conversation with her closest Friend.

'Dear Holy Spirit, I know you are my closest Friend. What Martins and I feel for each other, is it real or mere infatuation?' she asked. 'Soon he will be home for the holidays. Please strengthen

us so we will be strong and focused on your plans
for us,' she prayed.

She fell silent, thinking of the prayer she had just
said. Then, that Voice that spoke quietly but with
strength spoke within her. *'James 1: 12-17.'*

She picked up her Bible, flipped the pages to the
book of James and read, *'Blessed is the man that
endureth temptation: for when he is tried, he shall
receive the crown of life, which the Lord hath promised
to them that love him. Let no man say when he is
tempted, I am tempted of God: for God cannot be
tempted with evil, neither tempteth he any man: But
every man is tempted, when he is drawn away of his
own lust, and enticed. Then when lust hath conceived,
it bringeth forth sin: and sin, when it is finished,
bringeth forth death. Do not err, my beloved brethren.
Every good gift and every perfect gift is from above,
and cometh down from the Father of lights, with whom
is no variableness, neither shadow of turning.'*

Jina was awed by those words. God had just
responded to her prayers. She knelt down and
began praying more intensely. 'Yes, every good

and perfect gift comes from God. Martins is a good and perfect gift from God. He will not lead me astray,' she prayed. 'We will serve God together in righteousness; he will get to enjoy this unique relationship I enjoy with the Holy Spirit daily.'

She prayed intensely until she knew she had conquered, emerged victorious; there was no more fear! She had the nature of God, which was righteousness. She inherited it when she became born again, and she was bold and fearless now.

'Yes, perfect love drives out fear,' came that inner Voice.

She had heard that statement before but didn't know where it was written in the Bible. She picked up her Bible again, closed her eyes and muttered, 'Dear Holy Spirit, You just spoke to me again. Please tell me where I can find this statement in the Bible so I will study it for myself. You are my Instructor, my Teacher and my Friend. Please tell me where it is,' she concluded.

'*1 John 4:18,*' she heard again in a whisper.

She rushed to that part of the Scripture and found the statement. 'There is no fear in love; but perfect love casteth out fear: because fear hath torment. He that feareth is not made perfect in love.'

She read it repeatedly until it sank into her spirit. She declared it to herself often, kept her mind on it until the statement swallowed up her fears and uncertainty.

****

Jina was back early from the youth fellowship outreach. Her mother wasn't home. She had told her she would be going to the market to get groceries for the Wilsons.

Not having much to do, Jina lay down on her bed, took her daily devotional and flipped through some pages. An article titled FLEE caught her fancy. She stopped to read it.

Genesis 39 vs.12 (MSG):
"*She grabbed him by his*

cloak, saying, 'sleep with me!' He left his coat in her hand and ran out of the house."

The body of the article explained the verse and all that Joseph went through because he fled from the temptress. Joseph was doubted, the people he looked up to and trusted did not believe his innocence, they all termed him guilty and he was incarcerated for a crime he knew nothing about.

At the end of the article was the prayer:

'Lord, help me to flee when I should and give me the grace to believe the innocence of the innocent when the need arises, in Jesus' name, Amen.'

Jina dwelt on the prayer until she fell asleep with the devotional lying across her chest. Some noise outside woke her up. She sat up and listened. The voices were quite loud and she picked out Mrs.

Wilson's voice, heard Alfreda sobbing, but another voice—a third voice—filled her mind with confusion. It sounded so much like Martins' voice. But he wasn't back yet. At least, he hadn't informed her that he was home. She sat up in her bed and listened hard as the voices continued to tower over each other. She tiptoed to the window, parted the curtain slightly to have a clearer view, and her heart melted at the sight before her.

Martins stood looking confused, with part of his shirt torn, while Alfreda and her mom each had a piece of Martins' torn shirt. They were all talking at the same time with loud voices so that Jina had to strain her ears to make out what they were saying. She observed that Martins was visibly angry and shaking. She hadn't seen him like that before. He was making so much effort to explain himself to Old Soldier, who had run from his duty post to the scene of the commotion.

Mrs. Wilson, shouting at the top of her voice to drown Martins' voice, screamed, 'He is a worthless rapist! I caught him trying to rape my Alfreda!'

Alfreda turned pale as she stared at her mother in shock. 'Mom!'

Mrs. Wilson shot her a horrific glance. 'Shut up and thank God I came in at the right time to wrench his filthy hands off you,' she scolded her daughter.

Martins tried vainly to let his voice be heard. When it appeared he was making no headway, he tapped Old Solider on the shoulder and used the back of his left hand to wipe the perspiration from his forehead. Jina heard him sniff back threatening tears as he walked away from the scene without a backward glance.

'I believe the young man,' Jina heard Old Soldier say to Mrs. Wilson. 'It's only a madman that will come into a compound like this and try to rape a young mistress, and he doesn't seem mad to me,' he mused further. 'That young man doesn't strike me as a madman or a drug addict, so why would he do such a thing?' Old Solider continued shaking his head vigorously.

'Oh, shut the hell up!' Mrs. Wilson yelled. 'What do you know? Are you trying to cover up for him or should I believe you connived with him to carry out this act?'

Alfreda sat on the staircase holding her head in her hands and sobbing. Old Solider glared at Mrs. Wilson with so much hatred and clenched fists. He exhaled gradually, turned and walked back to his duty post.

'I never want to see that bastard on this premises again. If I do, you will lose your job,' Mrs. Wilson spat out after him.

He didn't as much as turn an inch to acknowledge that he'd heard her. He walked on in silence.

Mrs. Wilson half-dragged Alfreda up. 'Stand up, you fool,' she said through clenched teeth. Lowering her voice, she added, 'Why will you always allow Jina have all the best things around?'

'Mom, Martins loves Jina and not me. I can't force myself on a man who has no love for me,' Alfreda said meekly, tears streaming down her cheeks.

'Shut up, you fool,' her mother scolded. 'I am your mother and I know what's good for you. Now, I'm telling you, Martins is good for you. You must go get him by all means,' she lectured.

'Mom, I can't. Besides, you just warned that he shouldn't be allowed into this compound so how am I. . .'

'Shut up and get inside, and let me think of another strategy,' Mrs. Wilson interrupted her daughter, who merely shrugged and rested her back on the wall.

'Where are those letters and gift items?' she asked Alfreda.

'They are in my room,' she replied, wondering what her mother was up to this time.

'Ensure no one knows about them. When I come up with a good plan, I will let you know. Now get inside,' she commanded her daughter.

As Alfred went into the house, Mrs. Wilson picked up the pieces of Martins' shirt before going inside too, shutting the door loudly.

****

'What was that?' Jina asked herself. 'Was that drama real or was I dreaming?'

She touched her forehead to check if she was running a temperature, but everything appeared normal. She couldn't believe what she had just witnessed. Anger and disappointment welled up within her. So Martins was back and didn't as much as care to let her know he was around. What had he been doing in Mrs. Wilson's house? When did he arrive? What letters and gift items was Mrs. Wilson talking about? Many questions flooded her mind, but there were no answers. Was Martins seeing Alfreda too? Had he just been deceiving Jina all along? Who would volunteer answers to these questions?

She tucked her hands in her jean pockets and paced the floor of their tiny apartment many times, trying to calm her nerves and find answers to her questions. She sat down on her bed, lowered her face into her palms and exhaled loudly.

A taxi drove into the premises. She stood and saw her mom come out of the taxi. The driver leaped out to help her bring the bags out from the boot. She knew she should go out and help her mother carry the bags into the main house, but she didn't want Mrs. Wilson to know she had been at home when that drama unfolded. She sat back on her bed and closed her eyes to shut the memories out, but it was difficult. She kept reliving the whole episode until her mother stepped into their apartment.

'Jina, are you all right?' her mother asked.

'Yes, Mother . . . no,' she stuttered.

'Tell me about it and don't play big girl with me,' her mother said over her shoulder as she washed her hands under the running tap at the sink and proceeded to wipe them with a hand towel.

'Mom, do you think Martins is in love with Alfreda?' She spilled the question before she had the chance to rephrase it.

Mrs. Jordan didn't answer immediately. She had known a day like this would come but never knew it would be this soon and in this manner. Old Solider had told her how Mrs. Wilson had been intercepting their letters. He also told her how Mrs. Wilson had told everybody that cared to listen that Alfreda was a better wife material for Martins than Jina.

'Jina, the blessing of God makes rich and adds no sorrow,' Mrs. Jordan started. 'If Martins is for you, if he is God's perfect will for you, none can take him away,' she said, feeling very sad for her daughter.

'Mom, Martins is home,' Jina said quietly.

'How did you know?' her mother asked.

'I saw him with Alfreda and Mrs. Wilson this afternoon.' Her voice cracked with emotion and tears welled up in her beautiful eyes. Mrs. Jordan was quiet for a while, thinking of what to tell her daughter.

'Mom,' Jina continued, with the tears now streaming down her face, 'how do we know God's gifts to us?'

Mrs. Jordan swallowed the lump in her throat and said, 'Every good and perfect gift is from the Lord. He gave us His nature of righteousness so we can be like Him and discern the good and perfect gifts He gives us.'

'Martins is good and perfect for me so he is God's gift to me,' Jina said, more to herself than her mother.

'Yes, but you don't need to fight over a man with anybody, more so with Alfreda, who is like a sister to you,' Mrs. Jordan advised. Jina looked at her mother with a tear-stained face and resolved within her to do the right thing.

She had the nature of God, which is righteousness; she wouldn't act otherwise. She would handle this matter with the wisdom of God and be sure she made God proud of her.

No man was worth losing her salvation for, so she would not throw it away for any man, Martins inclusive. No man would love and take care of her like God. God gave her all that she owned, including the ability to stand bold at all times before God—the Maker of all things! This was what righteousness did for the believer. They were able to stand before God without any feeling of inferiority or shame; they are bold, because they have God's nature. Nothing and no one could condemn them.

With this resolve, Jina stood up, gave her mother a hug and told her that all would be well. She assured her mother she wouldn't do anything silly, but at the same time she wouldn't allow someone else take away God's blessings for her.

Mrs. Jordan nodded, not knowing what else to say. She prayed silently that her daughter wouldn't do anything to destroy the working relationship she had with her employers.

CHAPTER FOUR

INSPIRATION

When Jina waited for days to hear from Martins but didn't, her anger turned to worry. Was he all right? Had his feelings for her changed? The annoying thing was, she couldn't find the right person to ask.

One day as she was coming back from her church activity, she ran into Alfreda by the gate.

'Hi Alfreda, how are you doing?' she asked.

'I'm great and you?' Alfreda replied.

'I'm doing well, thank you,' Jina responded.

She waited a little to see if Alfreda had something else to say to her, but when nothing more was forthcoming, she continued on her way to the house.

'Old Solider,' Alfreda called.

The security man came out and said something to Alfreda, who giggled and said 'thank you.'

Jina had a feeling something was going on but couldn't pinpoint what. She saw Alfreda enter Old Soldier's lodging and emerge with a brown envelope and a cellophane bag. Jina watched Alfreda head towards the main house and as Alfreda came near the house, Jina came back outside and asked, 'Did the postman come today?'

'No . . . em . . . yes,' Alfreda stuttered, trying to hide the envelope from Jina.

Jina could have sworn she saw her name written in Martins' handwriting on the envelope, but she couldn't prove it. Both young women glared at each other for a while and parted without another word.

What was happening? Jina kept asking. She couldn't even talk to anybody about it. Her mother would have been the best person, but after their last discussion on that issue, she didn't want to head that way again. She sat on her bed, held her head in her hands and shut her eyes to get her mind to steady.

'*Pray,*' that soft Voice said to her.

As she opened her mouth, she could make no sound. Tears spilled down her cheeks, flowed down freely from her eyes and she made no effort to wipe them.

'Lord, please I need your guidance here. I have a feeling that those things Alfreda has were mine. Yet I can't confront her. How do I go about this, dear Lord,' she prayed, using the back of her left hand to wipe her nose.

After prayers, she took her church notepad and opened it, and two scriptures stood out from the page she opened: Habakkuk 2: 3-4 and Hebrews 10: 35-39.

Then Jina grabbed her Bible and opened the two scriptures that she saw in her notepad. She speed-read them the first time, then went through them a second time, more slowly this time. She got the message! The Lord was telling her to be patient. She closed the Bible and stood up, hands on her hips. The Lord had said she should be patient and that was exactly what she was going to do. She would wait patiently!

Few days later, Jina was alone in the house feeling bored and lonely. She walked to the window and peered outside. The scene where Mrs. Wilson stood accusing Martins of trying to rape Alfreda flashed through her mind. She shuddered at the venom she had seen on her face and heard in her voice. She wished she could get to the root of the whole matter, but didn't know how to go about it.

Old Solider! she thought.

But would he be willing to help? Wasn't he the one who gave Alfreda the gifts and letter Martins sent to her? But there was no harm in trying, yes . . . but she didn't want to get hurt further . . .

Yet she saw herself opening the door and heading towards Old Soldier's lodging.

'Good afternoon, sir,' she greeted on getting to her destination.

'Little Ma'am, good afternoon,' Old Solider responded cheerily.

'Em . . . I'm sorry . . . I wish . . .' she stammered, not knowing where or how to state her mission.

The old man looked at her with much concern. He went behind the door of his house and pulled out a thick envelope from an overall hanging there. He handed it over to her and waved her off quickly.

She took the envelope and half-raced to their apartment. She quietly opened the door and as soon as she was in the safety of their apartment, she heard Mrs. Wilson's voice talking with Old Solider. Well, thank heavens she was already home. She breathed.

Her heart was thumping with anticipation as she opened the envelope. It was from Martins. She read it repeatedly, tears sometimes blurring her vision. Why was this happening to her? Why couldn't she freely have the man she truly loved and admired? Many questions raced through her mind but there were no answers to them.

****

Martins loved her, but couldn't express same openly for he feared Mrs. Wilson`s wrath against Jina and her mother. They could be hurt if she found out that he was still communicating with them. He was being coerced into a relationship with Alfreda or risk losing his late father's property. Mrs. Wilson has talked Martins' uncle into this scheme, it seemed. His reason was that Jina was not of Martins' class; she was a commoner, the daughter of a nobody. Martins was going back to Canada in the next couple of days with Alfreda.

However, he said she was not to worry, quoting Romans 8:28, '*And we know that for those who love God all things work together for good, for those who are called according to His purpose.*'

'All things work together for my good—does it include giving up the only man I have ever loved?' she queried no one in particular.

Tears welled up in her eyes again as she read the line where Martins wrote that she should be of good behaviour and always remember her labour of love and prayers for him would not be in vain.

'What is he talking about?' she muttered to herself.

Her eyes went back to the last paragraph of the letter:

> We are each other's inheritance, yes, each other's heritage from the Lord!

He'd gone ahead to list what heritage meant to him: Healing, Excellence, Righteousness, Inspiration, Truth, Abundant life, Grace, and Eternal life.

He had also assigned scriptures to each of the words. *Typical of Martins*, Jina thought. What he wrote under the word 'inspiration' amazed her. He said Christ's love for him and Jina's tender love inspired him no end. He told how this love made him not to fall prey to Mrs. Wilson's antics the last time he visited their compound. He wrote:

`I came to see you, my tender Jina, but ran into a wolf! Mrs. Wilson lured me into her house on the pretext that you were working in her bedroom. While I sat waiting for her to call you as she had promised, she emerged, pulled up her dress and asked if I liked what I saw. I said no and stood up to leave. At this point, she called on Alfreda, who came out of her room crying.' I was wondering at what both of them were up to when Alfreda came clinging to me so hard. As I tried to extricate myself from her grip my shirt tore and she had a piece of the torn shirt as evidence that I had come to rape her.

This is the story they narrated to my uncle and the police and that is what got me into the situation I am in now; loving you but being forced to take another. I am continually inspired by God's word and love embedded within us.

I think of Jeremiah 29: 11 which says, "'*For I know the plans I have for you,' says the lord.*" 'They are plans for good and not for disaster, to give you a future and a hope'" and Hebrew 13:6, "*So we can say with confidence, 'The Lord is my helper, so I will have no fear. What can mere people do to me?'*" These scriptures strengthen and comfort me.'

Jina didn't know whether to scream or to keep quiet. She was filled with so much pain and agony, yet she observed a tiny streak of strength coming from within and she called it the same thing Martins called it, 'Inspiration.'

CHAPTER FIVE

TRUTH

Jina buried herself in the study of God's Word. She devoured chapter after chapter each day as the Bible became her only companion. She didn't have many activities outside her home for she was done with schooling now and awaiting her results. She had no real friends in the sense of the word. Martins had gone back to Canada with Alfreda, so she was all by herself now. The only time she got to go out was when she had church activities or when she accompanied her mother to the market to buy groceries for Mrs. Wilson's household. Otherwise, she would be home, armed with her Bible and a notepad.

In the course of her meditation and study of God's word, she encountered the reality of God's word. She found that the word of God was able to produce what it talked about in any given situation. God's Word was truth and this truth when taken in its totality delivered divine inheritance, divine estate and proper placement in life. It changed the believers' levels and caused God's dream and purpose to be fulfilled in them.

Jina discovered the efficacy of God's word as she applied it to her daily living; her once boring life began to glow. Her happiness and excitement became so infectious that even Mrs. Wilson wondered at her most of the time. One evening, as she was coming back from a church activity, she met Irene, Martins' sister.

They hugged and chatted on a number of issues, neither of them wanting to be the first to talk about Martins for fear of how the other person would react. As they made to part ways, Irene's cell phone rang and it was Martins calling.

'Oh dear, you won't believe who I'm standing with,' Irene said with glee, after the pleasantries.

'Tell me,' Martins replied.

'No, you guess,' Irene teased.

There was a little hesitation on the other end of the line and finally Martins whispered, 'My tender Jina!'

Tears welled up in Irene's eyes as she felt the affection and torture in her brother's voice, 'Yes,' she whispered back, sniffing.

'Can I please talk to her?' Martins begged.

'Oh, why not?' Irene asked as she handed the cell phone to Jina.

'Hi Martins,' Jina greeted calmly, though her heart raced frantically.

'My tender Jina,' Martins called out softly.

'How are you doing?' Jina asked, trying so much to subdue her quivering.

'I'm not doing well without you,' Martins replied.

'Please don't go there,' Jina begged.

'My heritage,' Martins called out softly, 'I lack words . . . just too overwhelmed with everything,' he said.

'Be strong, Martins. Keep your faith alive in God,' she encouraged.

'Sometimes it gets so difficult. Why is God allowing me to go through this kind of pain again?' Martins asked.

'Did you say again?' Jina asked.

'Yes, I felt so much pain when I lost both of my parents in one day. When I met you I was comforted and now I'm thrown into this pensive mood again,' Martins poured out in one breath.

'Please, Martins, don't make it harder for me to bear,' Jina begged.

'My tender Jina, take my number from Irene. I will send you some money so you can call me and we will talk at length, pray together and get God's thought on this please,' Martins instructed.

Typical of him, no time for negotiations over what he truly desired.

'And collect my email address as well. I'm not prepared to lose you, not for a million Alfreda's and Mrs. Wilsons,' he said amidst protests from Jina.

'Jina, we are each other's heritage from the Lord. I'm not married and will not marry Alfreda. God has better plans for us, that I'm very sure of,' he concluded.

'How is she?' Jina asked in a bid to take the attention off herself.

'I guess she should be fine. I haven't seen her for weeks,' Martins replied without interest.

'Did you say weeks? I thought you lived together,' she asked.

'Live together? As siblings, a couple or friends?' he asked.

'I. . .' Jina stuttered, but Martins interrupted her.

'Jina, you are the only one I ever want to live with,' he stressed.

'And where is she?' Jina asked, feeling bad for Alfreda.

'Please, let's talk about ourselves. I have an assignment for you, my tender shoot,' Martins said, changing the subject.

'Which is?' Jina asked obediently.

'Write and send to me twenty characteristics of God's word. Send it through my email address,' he said.

'What is it for?' Jina asked, wondering at the assignment.

'Personal,' Martins said and chuckled at the picture he saw in his mind of the expression on Jina's face.

'I will try. We have kept Irene waiting for long,' she reminded him.

'I'm sure she doesn't mind. She sure wants her only brother happy,' Martins said laughing.

'Do take good care of yourself,' Jina said.

'I will, my heritage, take care of you too… I love you dearly,' Martins replied.

'Thank you and I love you too,' Jina said, smiling.

'My tender shoot,' Martins called out. 'I'm expecting the mail,' he said.

'I will try,' Jina said, laughing.

She handed the cell phone back to Irene, who nodded her thanks and continued talking with her brother. When she was done, she brought out a piece of paper from her bag and wrote down Martins' email address and phone number. She handed the paper to Jina, who smiled her thanks, but doubted she would ever use those details.

'Thank you so much,' Jina said. 'I truly appreciate.'

'Oh, please don't mention it. God has a way of meeting us at the point of our needs,' Irene replied, giving her a hug.

'I think you are right,' Jina said shyly.

'Relax, everything will be fine. God won't allow what belongs to us to be taken away,' Irene encouraged.

'Thank you,' Jina said again.

'Martins got Alfreda admission in a college of journalism. She is living in the hostel and not with Martins, so relax,' Irene explained as if reading Jina's thoughts.

'Oh, thank you. I really can't thank you enough,' Jina replied, relieved.

'Martins loves you, that I am sure of. Now get going, girl. Remember to do the assignment he gave you,' Irene said, giving her a slight shove.

Jina thanked her again and walked away, wondering at the beautiful turn of events. She got home in high spirits as usual, but something about the twinkle in her eyes caught her mother's attention. Since the incident involving Martins and the Wilsons, her mother had avoided mentioning Martins to Jina for fear of how she would react.

Even when Alfreda left for Canada with Martins, they did not discuss it. Each person handled her pain and feelings alone.

'You are in such high spirits today,' Mrs. Jordan commented during dinner.

'I have always been this way,' Jina replied, smiling.

'Yes, but there is an unusual twinkle in your eyes today,' her mother pointed out.

Jina merely smiled and shrugged her shoulder. 'The joy of the Lord has always been my strength,' she responded, evading her mother's scrutiny.

'Tell me about it,' her mother nudged.

'Oh! Mom, there's nothing there to tell,' Jina said as she scooped some food into her mouth.

'You are not a good liar,' her mother insisted. 'You don't know how to pretend, so please out with it,' the woman continued.

'Ok, Mom,' Jina said, smiling. 'I met Irene, Martins' sister, on my way back from the church. We chatted on a number of issues and em . . . that's it,' she explained, scooping another spoonful of vegetable salad into her mouth.

'Is that all?' her mother asked with eyebrows raised.

'Oh Mother! You're impossible,' Jina exclaimed, laughing. She dropped her spoon and gave her mother a detailed account of all that happened that evening. 'But, Mom, I don't intend to use those contact details of his,' she said, not wanting to offend her mother.

'Why ever not?,' her mother asked, throwing Jina off balance.

'Mom, you told me to leave him for Alfreda, and both of them are living in Canada now,' she explained.

'I don't remember telling you to leave him for Alfreda. Rather, I said not to fight with your sister over a man. It's obvious he loves you genuinely, so go for what's yours,' her mother lectured.

'Mom!' Jina called, surprised.

'Yes, you heard me very well,' her mother replied, gazing into her awe-struck eyes.

'Is there something you are not telling me?' Jina asked her mother calmly.

'Well, let's say you finish up your meal and get to work doing the assignment Martins gave you,' her mother said, rising from her chair.

Jina was amazed. She gazed at her mother for a while, shrugged her shoulders and resumed her meal, albeit pensively.

****

Jina had just finished writing the letter she wanted to send to Martins. She read through again and checked through the twenty characteristics of God's word she wrote.

'Why in the world does he want this? And why didn't he find them out himself?' she asked herself again.

Anyway, she read the write up and was amazed at what she had written:

God's word grows, Acts 19:20

God's word is full of power and can make you what it talks about, John 6:63

God's word heals; it's an antidote for sickness, Proverbs 4:22

It delivers us from evil and delivers our inheritance to us, Colossians 1:13

It is the perfect recipe for success, Joshua 1:8

It transforms and prospers, Romans 12:2

It is efficient, effective and never returns void when sent forth, Isaiah 55:11

It is excellent and sufficient, requiring no addition or subtraction, Revelation 22:18-19

It is the power of God unto salvation, Romans 1:16

It is a life giving seed, 1 Corinthians 3:6-7

It is faithful, Titus 1:9

It is the word of life, Philippians 2:16

It is the word of truth, 2 Timothy 2:15

It is God's inspiration, 2 Timothy 3:16

It is good, holy and spiritual, Hebrews 6:5

It is the spiritual food full of nourishment, Mathew 4:4

It is the source of lasting joy, Luke 10:21

It is wisdom personified and it makes people wise, Psalm 119:100

It gives hope that doesn't make us ashamed, Romans 15:4

It burns like fire and it can smash the rock to pieces, Jeremiah 23:29.

As she read, she got more inspiration from her write up and began to describe God's word further to Martins:

> "God speaks words of power and knowledge to us. He gave us His Word so we can become His word, and His word on our lips is like Him talking. They will produce the same result. We are products of His word and His word sustains us. His word gives us our heritage from Him and helps us manage the blessings we get from Him. God's word is creative and curative!"

At this point, Jina kept her notepad aside, lifted her hands in worship to God as she experienced the power and presence of the Holy Spirit. She praised, prayed, prophesied and declared words of power over her life and affairs. When she was done, she headed to a Cyber café where the mail was typed and sent to Martins.

****

A few days later, she got a reply from Martins and the question that stood out from his reply was 'What was your experience while writing those characteristics? Tell me about it . . .'

She replied, explaining to him how she felt the presence of the Holy Spirit and how she worshipped and prophesied as she penned those characteristics.

His reply to her second mail amazed her. He wrote:

'My heritage, the experience you had was my reason for the assignment. I wanted you to look away from our situation and focus on God's word. The assignment is the only way I could have gotten you to do that for us. Now I'm relaxed knowing you are soaring high in the presence of God and keeping faith alive for our future together. My tender shoot, make God's word your stay and pray for us daily. The gates of hell will not prevail against the truth of God's word.

I love you endlessly,
Martins

CHAPTER SIX

ABUNDANT LIFE

While waiting for her call up letter to go for her one year national youth service, Jina got a job as an administrative assistant in a law firm. She was so committed to her duty that her employer took to her, citing her as an example to the other employees.

There was no longer a communication gap between her and Martins. They got in touch with each other often, the internet facilities in the law firm and the new mobile phone Jina bought with proceeds from her monthly allowance made this possible.

****

'I said I am going to Canada to see my daughter,' Mrs. Wilson shouted.

'And I said you are not going anywhere,' Mr. Wilson replied calmly.

'Why?' she asked.

'Because you are trying to ruin Alfreda! You forced her into a relationship and sent her off to a faraway country without my consent. Are you out of your mind, woman?' Mr. Wilson asked, livid with rage.

'She's my daughter and I know what's good for her,' Mrs. Wilson shot back.

'No, you don't. You are simply selfish and ruthless,' Mr. Wilson retorted.

Mrs. Wilson's shock was visible. She hadn't seen her husband this furious before. However, she quickly braced herself up and maintained her stance on the matter.

'Martins abandoned my daughter in a school all this while and you think there's nothing wrong with it,' she hurled at her husband.

'Is Martins not in school too? Besides, he is in love with someone else and you are forcing your daughter on him. Woman, get reasonable for once!' he fired back.

'He can't be in love with a mere housemaid, a nobody, a. . .'

'Shut your trap! Jina is as much my daughter as Alfreda is,' Mr. Wilson spat out angrily before he could stop himself.

'What did you say?' Mrs. Wilson asked in a hushed tone, her eyes frantically scanning for a chair to sit down.

'Yes, Jina and Alfreda are my daughters. The earlier we get things sorted out the better for everybody,' Mr. Wilson said calmly.

Mrs. Wilson supported her head with her hands and just gazed into space, thinking of what to do or say to hurt the man standing before her as he had hurt her.

'How did it happen?' she asked, not knowing if she truly wanted the answer or not.

'Mrs. Jordan was my secretary and we fell in love. I had the two girls with her, but my parents insisted I couldn't marry her because she was not as educated as they wanted my wife to be. I pleaded, but they refused and vowed to disown me and take away all that belonged to me if I didn't comply with their instruction.

'Then you came along . . . my mother arranged everything. I married you against my will. When years passed and you were unable to conceive, you suggested an adoption. As at that time Mrs. Jordan was already married to another man who died a few months after his marriage to her. The burden of catering for the two kids with no defined means of income was solely on her. You know, Alfreda was always sick as a child and Mrs. Jordan could hardly cope. I approached her for adoption, but she vehemently refused.

'One day, I visited them and found Alfreda almost dying. I couldn't stand it and I insisted I wanted to take her and care for her. I didn't want to lose any of my kids. She agreed on the condition that she had to be close by to ensure

Alfreda's safety and well being, hence her becoming our employee. Honestly, nothing intimate happens between us now. She feels I disappointed her; she is here because of our kids,' Mr. Wilson said with a sigh of relief. He felt as if a very heavy load had been lifted off his shoulders.

Mrs. Wilson stood up from where she sat, went to the reading table, picked up the phone and dialled a number.

****

Jina froze where she was washing the dishes in the main kitchen. It was usual for her to come around to help her mom with the chores when she wasn't at the office. So Alfreda was her sister all along and she hadn't known it! Her heart boiled over with anger. But who was she to get angry with God, her mother or her father? Though pained by the revelation she heard, she had to tread cautiously. She didn't want them to know she had heard anything, so she maintained her cool.

It was, in fact, a season of discoveries, for Jina resumed work the next day and made another discovery. The lawyer she worked for was the custodian of Martins' parents' will. She heard her boss discussing with Mrs. Wilson on the phone at work that day. Mrs. Wilson was insisting that all Martins' allowances be stopped until she came up with the next line of action. Barrister Elvis tried explaining to her how difficult it would be to do that but she was adamant.

When Martins complained to her about the hardships he was beginning to experience and how he couldn't explain why his allowances were delayed, Jina couldn't tell him.

She resorted to prayers. 'Lord, You promised to supply all our needs according to Your riches in glory. You promised to lead us to where there are green pastures. You promised to make all grace abound towards us. You are our sufficiency; we are taking You at Your words,' she prayed.

Before long there was a shift. Mrs. Jordan's monthly pay received a boost and Jina equally got a raise in her monthly allowance from her workplace. With this, she was able to get an enhanced version of her Mobile phone. Communication with Martins became a lot easier. She also thought of helping Martins out financially now. She knew he would resist it, but she would insist. She would tell him it's a loan, that he could repay it when he got a job, after his masters degree programme. With her mind made up, she decided to send Martins a mail requesting for his bank account details so she could transfer the money to his bank account.

Having sent the mail to Martins, she felt somewhat relieved. She still wanted to ask her mother about her paternity, though. She remembered the last time she raised the question several years back. Her mother had felt so pained and hurt that she told herself she would never bring up the matter again. But with what she had overheard from Mr. Wilson few days ago, there was a renewed hunger to know who her real father was. She would start by asking the mother the reason for the raise in her monthly allowance.

With her mind made up, she settled to work on the assignments that littered her table.

At the close of work, Jina got ready to go home. As she made to lock her office door, Barrister Elvis called her to come to his office. It was quite unusual. But he was her boss, so she went to see him.

'I have several important things to discuss with you,' her boss began, 'but you must promise me that you won't let anyone else hear them.'

Jina noticed the man was burdened with the weight of whatever it was he wanted to tell her.

'I promise,' Jina said reassuringly.

'My life is being threatened.' Barrister Elvis just dropped the statement, closed his eyes and breathed out loudly as if he had also dropped off a heavy load.

'What?' Jina asked almost in a whisper.

'Yes, it's true,' Barrister Elvis replied. 'Jina, I know you are a Christian, I know you pray and God answers you. Please pray for me,' he begged.

'Shouldn't you be talking to the police instead of me?' Jina asked.

'No, I have done too many wrong and hidden things with the person involved to go to the police,' he explained.

Jina shifted uncomfortably in her chair but quickly regained her composure. 'Ok, so where do you want me to come in now?' she asked her boss.

'Take this file and read through the contents carefully. Store it in a secure place so if anything happens to me you will tell the world my own side of the story,' he said, handing her a big, bulky brown envelope.

Jina hesitated, but she took the file. As she made to stand up, Barrister Elvis spoke.

'Be very careful. Mrs. Wilson is a deadly viper. Don't let her know you work here otherwise you will become another one of her targets,' he warned.

'Mrs. Wilson?' Jina asked in shock.

'Yes. Don't say I didn't warn you,' he repeated.

Jina was transfixed on her chair. She didn't know whether to drop the file and run for her life or to thank her boss for the advice. As she was still in her state of indecisiveness, the security man tapped lightly at the door.

'Sir, Mrs. Wilson is here to see you. The receptionist has closed, that's why I had to come and inform you myself,' he said.

'Goodness me!' the boss exclaimed.

'Jina, you have to leave here fast, but by which way?' he asked no one in particular.

'Mr. Lucas, I need your help. I don't want Jina to be seen by Mrs. Wilson, how do we do that?

Think and fast, too!' he said, irritated at the whole turn of events.

'What about the security exit from your toilet? Sir, maybe she can use it,' Mr. Lucas suggested.

Both men shoved Jina towards the toilet door. Hardly had she entered the toilet than the door to Barrister Elvis' office flew open and Mrs. Wilson came in angry that she was left unattended to outside.

Meanwhile, Jina headed in the direction of the security exit, but it was locked. In their haste, neither of the men had remembered the key. She thought of going back to her boss's office, but the sound of Mrs. Wilson's voice warned her that she might not live to tell the story. She stood in her boss's toilet wondering what she had gotten herself into.

****

The security man remembered the security exit was always locked and beads of perspiration formed on his forehead. He quietly signalled to his boss and Barrister Elvis nearly passed out with fright thinking what might happen to Jina should Mrs. Wilson find her around the office, especially with the documents she had with her.

'I want to use your restroom , after that, we will leave for our date,' Mrs. Wilson said and headed towards the toilet door.

'Sorry, Ma'am, the toilet tap is bad. I was to call the plumber this morning, but his lines were switched off,' the security man said.

'So?' Mrs. Wilson asked, looking at Barrister Elvis for some explanation.

'Lucas, please take her to the administrative officer's toilet while I lock up,' Barrister Elvis said.

Mrs. Wilson hesitated. 'I can manage. Let's go,' she said to Elvis.

'You're sure?' the barrister asked.

'Yes,' she replied, picking up her handbag which she had earlier dropped on the table.

'Lord, I thank you for this situation didn't take you unawares,' Jina prayed. 'Shield me from the evil plans of the enemy. Keep me safe and I will remain grateful to you all my life,' she muttered and sat down on the toilet seat as her legs seemed to be giving way from the whole stress.

When she heard the click of her boss's door as they trudged out, she exhaled in relief and stood, pacing the floor, hoping and praying they remembered she was still there. After what seemed like an eternity, she heard the security man's voice calling out softly to her.

'Yes, I am in here,' she replied.

The door opened quietly and she emerged into the now dark office with the security officer's torch light providing little illumination.

'I'm sorry, Miss Jina,' he apologised. 'Oga gave me this for your transport fare as it's really late to walk home now,' he said, offering her some money.

'Thank you, but he shouldn't have bothered. I have my transport fare with me,' she said.

'All the same, it's yours,' he said, still offering her the money.

'In that case, let's share it,' she said and just then her phone rang. It was Martins. She was supposed to call him about an hour earlier. In the midst of the drama, it had skipped her memory.

'Hi, Martins! Please I'm so sorry but I'm still in the office. I will call you as soon as I get to the house, please,' she apologised.

'Still in the office? Are you all right? Is everything ok?' Martins asked with so much concern.

'Yes, please, let's talk later,' she replied.

'I love you, my tender shoot,' he called out before hanging up the call.

Jina took a note from the three notes the security officer was offering her and mouthed her thanks. The man protested, but she nodded her head, indicating it was all right, and headed briskly towards the exit door.

****

She met her mother by the gate looking worried as she got out of the taxi.

'I'm sorry, Mother,' she started, 'It won't happen again, please,' she apologised.

Her mother exhaled the worry that had mounted within her and hugged her.

'Thank God you are safe,' she said as she led her towards their apartment.

'Mr. Wilson and I were so worried about you,' her mother continued as they neared the door.

'You mean my dad and you?' Jina almost asked, but bit her tongue to stay quiet.

'You have quite a handful of stuff with you,' Mrs. Jordan noted, pointing at the envelope Jina had just dropped on her reading table.

'Yes, I brought some work home.' She spoke casually to take her mother's attention away from the envelope. 'Is dinner ready? I'm famished,' she said, changing the subject.

'I will get it while you freshen up,' her mother replied and headed towards the kitchen.

Jina thanked the Lord again for supplying all their needs according to His riches in glory. The month was nearly ending and she hadn't removed a dime from her last month's salary. She was planning to add this month's earnings to it and send it to Martins. God had awesomely been her source all this while and she would forever remain grateful.

'Of course, it's part of your inheritance as a child of God,' that small Voice within reminded her.

'You are right.' Jina smiled. 'I still need to be thankful for the inheritance,' she concluded.

She looked towards her wardrobe door where she had pasted Martins' acronym for heritage. 'A' stood for 'Abundance.' She nodded her head in agreement. *'Martins is so right and God is so faithful,'* she thought.

CHAPTER SEVEN

GRACE

Jina barely touched her dinner. She had a forlorn look, but she kept reassuring her mother that all was well. Her mother was beyond tempted to open the thick brown envelop her daughter came back with, for she presumed that inside it lay the reason for her daughter's moodiness.

After the quiet meal, her mother opted to clear the tables. Jina obliged, for she wanted to call Martins and apologise for missing their phone appointment. However, as she stood up to go make the call, there was a tap on the door. Both mother and daughter looked at each other with questions in their eyes.

'I will get it,' they both chorused and stopped.

Jina moved faster and grabbed the door handle just as her mother got to it.

'Oh!' they both chorused again when they saw Mr. Wilson standing there with both hands shoved into his trouser pockets.

'Did I intrude on anything?' he asked, looking at both women standing before him and feeling that jolt of guilt for keeping his first daughter in the dark about her paternity all these years.

'Yes,' Jina answered.

'No,' her mother said.

They had both spoken simultaneously.

'You can come in,' her mother said, while Jina glared at him with so much anger in her eyes.

'Your wife will not be happy if she finds you in our apartment this late,' Jina snorted out and walked back into the room. She headed straight to her bed, lay on it and faced the wall.

Mr. Wilson went after her, his hands still in his pockets.

"I didn't mean to upset you, Jina . . . baby,' he said softly. 'I am actually quite worried that my wife isn't home yet and her cell phone isn't going through,' he explained.

Jina cringed at his soft voice, but refused to let that get through to her. It had gotten through to her all these years of lies and deception, but now that she knew the truth she wasn't going to be fooled anymore.

'Have you called her cell phone?' Mrs. Jordan asked with concern in her voice, while eyeing Jina.

'Yes, but it's not going through. Moreover, she didn't go out with her car,' Mr. Wilson added, running his hand through his curly, thick black hair.

'That's strange,' Mrs. Jordan said.

'Maybe you should inform the police if you are so concerned about her whereabouts,' Jina shot offhandedly.

'Jina, please clear the table for me and wash the dishes if possible,' her mother said, trying to get her out of the room, for she was really acting strange tonight.

'Mother, I need to call Martins.' Jina objected to being shooed out of the room like some little brat.

'Suit yourself then,' her mother shot at her with anger audible in her voice.

Jina took one last glance at her mother and her employer—No! Her mother and father—and headed towards the table. She began clearing the table while her mother and Mr. Wilson stepped outside to continue their discussion concerning Mrs. Wilson's whereabouts.

'Do you think she knows?' Mr. Wilson asked, gesturing towards Jina in the house.

'Know what? Your wife's whereabouts? No. I don't think so. . .' Mrs. Jordan said, but Mr. Wilson cut her short.

'No! About us,' he explained, gesturing between two of them.

Mrs. Jordan froze, glanced behind her to ensure the door was closed and Jina wasn't within hearing range before responding.

'Why would you think so? Who would tell her, or did you?' she asked Mr. Wilson, apprehension in her voice.

'No, I didn't, but she is no longer a kid!' Mr. Wilson replied with his two hands shoved into his pocket.

'I pray she doesn't get to find out ever,' Mrs. Jordan said, still glancing towards the door to ensure it was still closed.

'Ever?' Mr. Wilson asked. 'I will say she doesn't get to hear it from the wrong source because I. . .'

'You what?' Mrs. Jordan cut in. 'Don't tell me you still intend to carry out the threat you made the other day,' she concluded, looking at him with pleading eyes.

'It's not a threat. I have had it up to my throat with my wife and I truly want out,' Mr. Wilson explained.

'I think we should leave that issue for now and focus on your wife's whereabouts,' Mrs. Jordan said, changing the topic.

She was feeling very uncomfortable with this discussion. She didn't want Jina losing confidence in her or even hating her for keeping such a secret from her. But it wasn't her fault she wanted the best for her children. If she had tried to handle them both by herself, then she might have lost Alfreda. And she wouldn't have wanted to risk that. She had acted on her motherly instinct. They were all alive, well and happy now. Things ought to remain that way.

****

Meanwhile, with the dishes all washed and stacked away, Jina dialled Martins' number. He picked it up at the first ring.

'My tender shoot,' he cooed into the receiver.

Jina beamed. 'Hi Martins. I'm sorry it took me this long to call,' she apologised.

'It's okay so long as you are all right,' he replied cheerily. 'So what's been happening with you?'

'Nothing much, just some little hitches here and there,' she replied.

They chatted on a number of things and she hinted that she had some money she wished to send to him, but he refused to accept money from her. After much argument, he unwillingly gave in because he was rather hard up. He had called his uncle several times to go find out what the issues were but the lawyer hadn't given them any good reason for his actions. Now, he needed money to offset some pressing bills and if God was gracious enough to provide for him through Jina then he might as well accept it.

Jina wanted to tell him about the brown envelope her boss gave her for safekeeping but felt there was no need since she hadn't even peeped into the envelope to know its contents. Besides,

Martins didn't know that Jina worked for Barrister Elvis, the custodian of his late father's will. But, why was Mrs. Wilson interested in making Martins and Irene suffer? It was not like they did anything to her, but she had always been on their case. Recently, she was mounting pressure on Martins to marry her daughter, Alfreda, who was, in fact, not even her daughter.

Speaking of Alfreda, who knew how she was doing over there in Canada? Martins swore they didn't stay in the same house and weren't in the same school. Alfreda lived in the hostel in another city from what she heard. Yes, Martins' financial crisis actually started the moment he stood his ground about Alfreda not living with him. Some more pieces of the jigsaw puzzle seem to be coming together to make sense, but Jina didn't want to press her thoughts further.

Martin's voice at the other end of the line brought her out of her reverie.

'I'm sorry, I missed that,' she said, feeling guilty for allowing her thoughts wander off while talking with Martins.

'It's okay. Are you feeling sleepy?' he asked with much concern in his voice.

'Not really, just a little distraction,' she replied.

'Want to share?' he asked, and she imagined his left eyebrow would be raised at that question.

She smiled to herself at the fond memory of him. 'Mrs. Wilson isn't home yet. Her cell phones aren't going through, and she left the house without her car,' she explained in one breath.

'Why? That's strange! Have you guys reported to the police yet?' he asked gently.

'Not really. Her husband said to wait a little longer before going off to the police,' she explained.

'It's well with her,' he said matter-of-factly.

They continued on a number of issues until they bade each other goodbye. Jina promised to go and make the money transfer to his account the next morning. When she ended the call, she was startled to see her mother standing by the door gazing at her with a not-too-pleasant look.

'Well?' she asked her mother with a shrug.

'Who are you sending money to?' her mother asked.

So she had heard her. *How long was she there listening to my conversation with Martins?* she thought angrily. She felt pissed that her mother had sneaked in on her while she was talking to a guy who meant so much to her.

'I asked a question,' her mother stated with irritation in her voice.

'It's personal,' Jina replied, sitting back on the bed.

'Jina, I am your mother and I demand an answer to my question right now!' Mrs. Jordan said through clenched teeth. She was surprised at herself for getting this upset with her daughter over this minor issue. She tried to figure out why she was this mad at her daughter but truly couldn't pinpoint what it was.

'And I said it's personal, Mom,' Jina replied with irritation rising in her voice, too.

'It is wrong to give a man money, especially when you aren't married yet,' Mrs. Jordan lectured.

Jina was in no mood for such lectures tonight, especially since her mother hadn't been a saint all this while. She had kept her father's identity from her, kept the fact that Alfreda was her younger sister from her, and who knew what more she had kept from her.

'Mom!' she barked with her hands raised, indicating that her mother should stop the lectures. 'I am in no mood for your lectures tonight.'

Mrs. Jordan was taken aback by this new Jina sitting metres away from her. The Jina Jordan that she knew would never raise her voice at her mother. Something was definitely not right somewhere!

Mrs. Jordan looked at her daughter in utter amazement, but she lacked the words to express her shock. She quietly moved into the kitchen to ensure the plates were already washed and stacked. In the kitchen, she still couldn't believe the incident of a few minutes earlier with her daughter. Should she ask her what the matter was? Should she just ignore it? A myriad of thoughts and questions raced through her middle-aged mind. She paused, took a deep breath. She suddenly exhaled sharply, her mind racing at a possibility that she just thought of.

'Oh God! No,' she muttered. 'It shouldn't be,' she said repeatedly to herself.

She had a flashback of her discussion with Mr. Alfred Wilson awhile back. But the door had been shut so Jina couldn't have heard them. But what if she had? What if Jina now knew her most guarded secret? Should she confront her, no, tell her the truth? She had a right to know who her father was. She had a right to know that Alfreda was her twin sister and not the daughter of her mom's rich employer. Should she tell her? No, if she did, too many things would go wrong. Too many lives would be affected negatively. Too many, yes, too many other issues would come up. She buried her face in her hands as she stood near the kitchen sink. Thoughts of yesteryears flooded her mind. She had thought this day would never come. She thought she had it all sealed and locked away in a forgotten cabinet. But, here she stood in the now of her life, with pain, memories and hurts of her past towering large in her mind and trying so much to dominate her. She was in love with Alfred Wilson, her boss. She knew they weren't in the same social class but she couldn't help it. The guy was nice to a fault. He took special interest in her, treated her far better than anyone else had ever done. It was too easy falling for him. Who wouldn't? she thought with a smile.

One day Alfred Wilson had walked into her tiny office. 'Miracle Evans,' he called softly, smiling as she fumed with anger.

'I am Mirabel Evans, sir, not Miracle,' she said through clenched teeth. This guy had a way of getting under her skin with the simplest things. She repeated it when he didn't say anything to her outburst. 'Mirabel Evans, please,' she said.

'No arguments,' he replied, holding up his two hands. 'But I have a right to call you whatever name I choose, don't you think so?' He breathed into her face as his face was inches away from hers.

There were too many knots tied within her, some in her stomach, some in her throat, preventing her from swallowing a lump that had formed there. She raised her face a little upward to gaze into those brown eyes that haunted her every night in her dreams, but that was her undoing. For as soon as that gesture was done, Alfred brushed her lips with his right thumb as the other four fingers held her chin in place. She shut her eyes tight, never wanting this moment to pass, never wanting to look into those gorgeous eyes before her.

'You are my Miracle,' he whispered huskily, and before she could flutter her eyes open to look at him, it happened—he brushed his lips against hers, making a smack sound between their lips, and then he disappeared as quickly as he came.

Her heart was thumping in her chest. She thought she would pass out. She gripped the sides of her table tightly to stop herself from falling out of the chair she was sitting on.

The moment froze and the whole world appeared to have frozen with it.

Alfred Wilson just kissed her!

Her face lit up with some colour. A wide smile spread across her face.

Oh God, why was she such a jerk? Why didn't she return the kiss? This had been her daily desire and nightily dream, yet when the moment came she had spoilt it.

'Mirabel Evans, you are a jerk,' she chided herself. She should have grabbed his face with both hands and kissed his lips till they hurt. She should have gotten up from her chair and wrapped her arms around him till they became one. Oh! Why didn't she? she mourned.

Weeks flew into months and her relationship with Alfred blossomed beautifully. Some envied her, some thought her stupid to think the Wilsons would accept her as their daughter-in-law. She didn't care about tomorrow or the future, what mattered were those moments she spent with Alfred.

One evening, as the two love-birds were nestling in their favourite park, each had something they wanted to discuss with the other but didn't know how to begin or how they would react.

'You go first, my Miracle,' Alfred urged her.

'No, you go first,' she said, gazing lovingly into his deep blue eyes.

He ran his fingers through his hair for the millionth time that evening, held her closer to his chest and shut his eyes. He didn't know how to begin, but he had to say it. This relationship had to end, his parents were so insistent on it. Either he ended it or he lost out on several other things, including the family inheritance and his relationship with his parents, especially his mother. She claimed she had gone too far with a family whose daughter was most suitable for him. He loved his mother way too much to hurt her, yet he loved his Miracle, too. He was at a crossroad. Tears of frustration stung his eyelids. He tried holding them but they spilled of their own accord, cascaded on his Miracle's earlobe and fell into her face.

She gazed up at him to see him weeping, and she didn't need any other telling. She knew the end had come for them. Now, it was her turn to cry. What would she do with the tiny bundle growing inside her? Should she tell him? No, she would bear it alone. The tiny bundle would remind her of him all the days of her life. She made up her mind not to tell him or anybody else. It was her cross and she would dutifully bear it alone. Their meeting ended with neither of them verbally expressing what was in his or her mind. She went home, packed her stuff and left town the very next morning. She couldn't bear to stay in the same city with him and not be able to hold his attention, talk more of working in the same establishment.

Little did she know that one can never really hide from one's shadow. She was literally forced on Engr. Jordan, an old man who was truly kind to her and fun to be with. But she had sealed her heart and so couldn't open it to him. A few months into the forced marriage, Engr. Jordan passed on and she was left to cater for the twins alone. She named the elder twin Jina, meaning 'one's self' in Swahili and 'the victorious' in Sanskrit. Her reason was that she was victorious despite all odds. The choice of languages stemmed from Alfred's love for foreign languages. The second and younger twin she named Abbie, meaning 'father's joy.' She truly looked like her father and Mirabel hoped that one day she would truly be her father's delight.

She wasn't surprised when Alfred Wilson showed up on her doorsteps few weeks after the death of her husband. His mission was to negotiate the adoption of one of the twins as his wife was medically declared infertile and he needed to be part of the twins' upbringing.

After many fights, arguments and visits, she gave in. Alfred and his wife adopted Abbie and renamed her Alfreda. A few weeks after the adoption, he fulfilled his promise by offering her a job as their nanny, housekeeper, chef rolled into one. They promised never to let the girls know they were blood relatives, not to talk of twins. Events had happened in the time past that almost unveiled the truth, but somehow her secret had remained secret.

When she met the Lord and gave her life to Christ, she wanted to spill her gut, but when Alfred reminded her of the several lives that would be affected and probably damaged in the process, she swallowed the bitter pill of secrecy once more. Now, it seemed the web she'd knitted was almost swallowing her up . . .

She gazed in the direction of her daughter, Jina. Their eyes met and held for a moment, and she knew without being told that Jina had found out the truth.

The question now was, who told Jina? How much did she know? What was Mirabel to do about it?

****

Jina woke up the next morning, said her prayers and was about to step into the bathroom when her mother came into the apartment. She greeted her warmly like the night before never happened.

'How's your night?' Mrs. Jordan asked her daughter.

'Beautiful,' she replied, 'and yours?'

'Good! Mrs. Wilson didn't return home last night,' Mrs. Jordan stated.

'Really? That's strange,' Jina opined.

'Yes, and her cell phone is still saying switched off,' Mrs. Jordan added.

'Has her husband informed the police?' Jina asked.

'No, he will do so this morning. He called a friend of his who is a security personnel and was told he could only report to the police formally after twenty-four hours of her disappearance,' she explained to her daughter.

'That's not good,' Jina stated. 'Anything could have happened to her before then.'

'You are right. We'll just pray she is safe wherever she is,' her mother said.

Jina shrugged and went into the bathroom. Her mind raced over different options. Should she tell her mother that she had seen Mrs. Wilson in her office late yesterday evening? Should she tell her mom about the envelope her boss gave her and the uncertainty she heard in his voice when he spoke to her about its content? No, she decided. After all, her mother kept things from her all these years. She should have her own little secret too. She smiled to herself.

'You are retaliating,' the Voice whispered within her.

Jina almost jumped, for she had temporarily forgotten about this Voice that was always her companion.

'No, I'm not,' she defended her actions.

'Yes, you are,' the Voice said. 'She didn't do well, but two wrongs don't make a right. You should forgive her and show her love and not pay her back in the same coin.'

Jina was torn between following her earlier laid out plans to keep to herself henceforth and yielding to the promptings of the Holy Spirit. She was hurt. Tears stung her eyes and she bit her trembling lips hard to stop them from quivering further. She sat down on the edge of the bathtub with her face buried between her two palms. She wept silently and prayed at the same time—for grace, strength and wisdom to handle this matter well.

'My grace is sufficient for you,' she heard. 'For My strength is made perfect in your weakness.'

'Thank You, dear Lord,' she breathed. She proceeded to take her bath and prepare for work.

****

'You are being very sluggish this morning, aren't you going to work?' Mrs. Jordan asked her daughter as she watched her move from one part of their apartment to the other. It was quite unlike her. Jina didn't usually need coercion to get ready for work.

'I'm dilly–dallying to ensure the bank is open when I leave. I intend to stop at the bank before getting to the office,' Jina explained.

'What's happening at the bank?' her mother asked, pretending not to remember last night's discussion.

'I have a transaction to make this morning before getting to the office,' Jina replied as coolly as she could manage.

'Jina Jordan!' her mother called sternly. 'Don't tell me you are still going to send money to that young man that you can hardly vouch for,' she said angrily.

'Mother, please,' Jina said, trying so hard to maintain her cool.

'I said you shouldn't do it,' her mother ordered. 'Jina Jordan, that young man is in a faraway country with Alfreda. You don't even know what's going on between them. You only know what he tells you, and his past isn't as wonderful as. . .'

'Mother!' Jina cut her mother short mid-sentence. 'If you say another negative thing about Martins, I will take it personal,' she said through clenched teeth. 'You don't know him, just like he doesn't know you. Your past, which you are trying so hard to cover, isn't as wonderful as you would like to paint it. Those actions and reactions in the past which you are trying to cover may far out-weigh his own past that you are trying to dig up. The same grace that saved you from your past also saved. . .' she fumed.

'Jina Jordan!' Mrs. Jordan called, cutting her short. She got up angrily from the edge of the bed where she sat but a loud bang on their door halted her further move. She walked briskly to the door and yanked it open without asking who was there as was her custom.

'Good morning, madam,' Old Soldier greeted sullenly, unlike himself.

'Good morning, Old Soldier, what's the matter?' Mrs. Jordan replied, making way for the security man to step into the apartment.

'Tragedy has struck,' Old Soldier lamented.

'What is it?' Mrs. Jordan asked with genuine concern.

'Some policemen are here,' the old man answered vaguely, getting his hearers more confused.

'What for?' Mrs. Jordan asked impatiently, peering outside to see if she could find anything unusual.

'Mrs. Wilson shot Barrister Elvis and shot herself too,' Old Soldier said, whining in pain as if he had witnessed it all happen.

'What?' chorused Mrs. Jordan and her daughter.

Mrs. Jordan rushed out of the apartment and headed for the main house.

Jina moved closer to Old Soldier and asked in a voice that she barely recognized, 'Where are they now?'

'Barrister Elvis bled to death as they were being rushed to the hospital, but Mrs. Wilson is in the ICU, critically injured,' Old Soldier explained.

Jina sat down on the floor and buried her face in her two hands as moans of anguish escaped her.

'No, Barrister Elvis can't die,' she sobbed.

The events of the previous evening replayed in her mind, over and over again. It dawned on her that Barrister Elvis must have seen his death coming, hence he had given her those documents for safekeeping.

****

Martins was uncomfortable after his discussion with Jina. He didn't like the idea of her sending him money. She should keep whatever she had for future use, she would need it. He reached out for the thousandth time to pick up his cell phone to call her back and tell her not to bother but he knew she would be upset. He knew her to be that stubborn when it came to things she truly wanted to do.

He called his sister instead and narrated his ordeal to her. Irene had always been a strong pillar to fall back on in situations like this. She had made his stay in Canada very comfortable and warm. She had always given him the reason and courage to go on even amidst challenges bigger than him.

After listening to him, she asked him not to bother calling Jina. She had to be allowed to follow her heart's leading. However, when the money came he shouldn't use it. He was to keep it safe so that peradventure she needed it he could send it to her.

Martins heaved a sigh of relief. Why hadn't he thought of this earlier? He thanked her profusely, asked after her job, health and the wellbeing of everybody else. After much 'here and there' gist, they bade each other goodbye and ended the call.

That night, Martins couldn't sleep. He tried reading but couldn't either. He resorted to praying. He prayed for a long time and finally drifted off to sleep. He woke up late the next morning to the ringing of his cell phone.

He thought it was Jina calling to tell him she had made the funds transfer. He picked up the call without looking at the screen to ascertain who the caller was. He answered sleepily, 'Good morning, my heritage.'

But the voice at the other end of the line didn't sound like Jina's and the person was sobbing. He sat up and took a closer look at the number that called him and discovered it was Alfreda.

'Hey, what's the matter?' he asked, rubbing his eyes to clear the remaining sleep from them.

'Did you hear anything from home?' she asked, still sniffing.

'Yes . . . no,' he replied in confusion. 'What happened?'

'I got an anonymous call from home telling me that my mother was involved in a ghastly motor accident and may not survive it. As I pressed further the line went dead. I have called my mother's phone several times but it isn't going through,' she sobbed.

Martins recalled vividly Jina's statement that Mrs. Wilson wasn't home and her cell phone was switched off. 'And your dad?' Martins asked, sitting up on the bed.

'His rang out without a response.' She cried harder.

'It may not be true, and even if it is, it may not be as bad as you are taking it,' he tried to console her, hoping truly that all was well.

'So why aren't they picking their calls?' she asked, still crying.

'Anything could have made them not to pick their calls, ranging from poor network to being busy,' he said in an attempt to calm her down. 'I spoke with Irene, my sister, and Jina yesterday, and they didn't tell me anything like that happened.'

He did not wish to bring up what Jina had said about Mrs. Wilson's unknown whereabouts.

'Ok, thank you,' she answered quietly. 'And how's Jina?'

'Very well, thank you,' Martins replied, stifling a yawn.

'I know you miss her very much.' It was more of a statement than a question.

'Hmm . . . you can say that again,' he replied, smiling at the thought of Jina.

The bracelet she gave him the first time he was coming to this country wasn't his size anymore. It now hung on a picture of the two of them, the picture they took during their high school graduation which he had enlarged and hung on the wall directly opposite his bed. Beneath their images was an inscription he had penned which read: *'Every good and perfect gift is from the Lord.'* Truly Jina was a good and perfect gift from God to him. She was the one who had stolen his heart with her tender love. No, she was the one who discovered he had a heart in the first place when no one believed he was capable of loving or showing any emotion. He smiled again—broadly this time—at her sweet memory.

Alfreda's voice at the other end of the line brought him back to reality.

'I'm sorry,' he apologised, for he hadn't heard what it was she had just said.

'It's okay . . . I was saying that trying to grasp a hold of what was never yours gets you very hurt in the end,' she repeated.

'Hmm . . . nice philosophy, but I don't see how that fits into our conversation,' he replied.

'My mom is still pushing me to get hooked to you. I admire you, though I did all she asked me to do to make her happy. But I know I was never going to get you, for you are truly in love with Jina,' she explained.

Martins was taken aback at her outburst. 'Interesting,' was the only thing he could say. 'So why are you telling me all these now?' Curiosity had gotten the better part of him.

'Just in case what they said about my mom is true, I'll want to apologise on her behalf, and mine too,' she responded calmly.

'Apology accepted, but I assure you that your mom is hale and hearty, so don't entertain any fear,' he told her.

'Thank you, but please promise me you won't hurt Jina. I love her like my sister, but my mom won't allow me to express it,' she confided in him.

'It's okay,' Martins said, still wondering at where this conversation was heading to. 'By the grace of God, Jina is very safe with me. I love her beyond words.'

'Okay then, do have a great day ahead. I will make some more attempts to see if I can get any information from home,' she said, signing off.

'Thanks, I wish you the same. I will call home, too. Cheers,' he responded and hung up.

As he dropped his cell phone on the bedside table, he wondered if what Alfreda heard was true or false.

But who could have made the call? He'd forgotten to ask her, was it a male or female voice she heard. Could it be true? Was Jina hiding it from him? Had Jina merely told him that story last night so as not to get him worried? Should he call Jina now? But he didn't want her thinking he was calling because he desperately needed the money she was going to send to him.

While still pondering on this, his cell phone rang again. This time it was Uncle Marc! Martins was surprised for his uncle had hardly spoken to him since the the false rape incident . He picked up the cell phone and responded to the greetings of Uncle Marc. Mr. Marc inquired of his well-being and told him without much ado that he would be sending him some money later that day. Martins was amazed at this sudden change but still thanked his uncle for his kind gesture.

A little while later Martins' phone beeped and it was his bank notifying him of funds transfer from Uncle Marc. Martins quickly typed an SMS to him to acknowledge the receipt of the funds and to show his appreciation once more.

He made a mental note to call Jina to tell her not to bother sending the money because of the one he received from his uncle. While on this, his cell phone began to ring again. As he reached for it and saw the caller, his heart skipped some beats. He *knew* that there was something wrong. He picked it and Mr. Alfred Wilson spoke from the other end of the line. After a few pleasantries, he told him that Mrs. Wilson had been shot and was presently in the ICU. He asked him to please relay the information to Alfreda.

****

Jina brought out the brown envelope she came back with the night before and began going through the contents one after the other. Her mother had gone with Mr. Alfred Wilson to the hospital where Mrs. Wilson was rushed to.

She saw things that made her weep, made her angry and hurt her deeply. How could she have worked with Barrister Elvis all this while and not known who he truly was? Barrister Elvis had known everything about her and Martins. He had known everything about Martins' parents and their deaths.

She found out that Mrs. Wilson had masterminded that because Martins' father refused to marry her. What a callous soul! She had made Barrister Elvis stop sending money to Martins unless Martins agreed to marry Alfreda. Barrister Elvis had been the custodian of Martins' parents' will and the bulk of Martins' late father's wealth was still under his control until Martins became twenty-five years old.

Jina wept herself sore when she found out the amount of wealth Martins' father had left. And to imagine that his children were barely getting by because of a wicked woman and a corrupt legal adviser!

Tears of anguish and pain flowed freely down her cheeks as she read how Martins' parents were shot dead with their legal adviser in the know.

What should she do with these documents? Should she tell Martins about them? Should she burn them and pretend she didn't know a thing? Should she inform her mother? Her mother! Ah .. . she was angry with her because she was determined to send Martins some money. But with the latest development, she began to wonder if she should listen to her mother. With Barrister Elvis dead and Mrs. Wilson hospitalized, what would become of her mother and herself?

No, she chided herself, Martins was in a foreign country and needed money to cope with the situation of things there. But then she didn't think she could make it to the bank today with the way things were at the moment.

****

Mrs. Jordan was in the hospital to see Mrs. Wilson. She wasn't allowed into the ICU, only

Mr. Wilson was. She sat at the hospital's reception and reflected on the events of the previous evening and this morning and blamed herself for insisting that Jina shouldn't send money to Martins. She had even talked about Martins' past, a past that she knew little or nothing about. Looking around her in the hospital environment, she realised that the good one did to a fellow human being was the best investment. For, those were what one would be remembered for when a day like this came for such a one. If she had a cell phone she would have called Jina to apologise to her and ask her to go ahead and do what she wanted to do for her friend.

Yes, she would also tell her that she was right. The same grace that saved her from her sordid past equally saved Martins and any other believer. The grace of God didn't discriminate. Once a person accepted it, it worked wonders and made all things new. The same level of grace that saved the worst criminal saved the so-called white liar. Titus 2:14 (MSG) said, '*He offered Himself as a sacrifice to free us from a dark, rebellious life into this good, pure life, making us a people he can be proud of, energetic in goodness.'*

Grace truly did not discriminate; she shouldn't have said those things about Martins and now she was regretting them.

CHAPTER EIGHT

ETERNAL LIFE

Mrs. Wilson's condition was bad, but the doctors assured her husband that she would pull through. So many issues were coming up from this singular act of his wife's desperation. He knew she was bad, but nothing had prepared him for the rude shock he kept getting daily on account of her wicked nature. She was not just an adulterer but a murderer, too. She planned and masterminded the killing of Martins' parents simply because Martins' father refused to marry her. She prevailed on Barrister Elvis to stop sending funds to Martins in Canada until he married Alfreda. Eventually, she executed Barrister Elvis—murdered the man in cold blood—because she felt he was backing out of their deals. She turned Martins and Irene to orphans, and now she had made Barrister Elvis's young wife a widow, and his little son fatherless!

Mr. Wilson rubbed his temple with both hands and stood up from the chair where he'd been sitting for only-God-knew how long. He thrust his two hands in his trouser pocket and paced round the small room where his so-called wife lay motionless except for the slight up and down heaving of her chest indicating that she was still alive. He wished for the hundredth time that he could end this whole misery by unplugging the oxygen mask that covered her nostrils and pulling out all other life support gadgets that she was connected to.

The vibration of his cell phone in his pocket pushed the malicious thoughts away from his mind. He brought out the cell phone and gasped as he realised he was almost two hours late for picking Alfreda from the airport. He hastened towards the door while taking his call. To his relief and surprise, Alfreda was already in the hospital premises and wanted to know which direction she was to take.

He quickly dashed out and walked through the long corridor outside under the blazing sun. He caught a glimpse of her under a shrub with her back towards him as she didn't know which way he would be emerging from. Relief washed through his stuffy mind for the first time since this whole weird drama began unfolding. Alfreda was here, alive and well. And this would be the best time to bring his family together and ask his twin daughters to forgive him and their mother for their selfish acts.

He strode as fast as his legs could carry him to where his daughter stood. She hadn't changed much, still her beautiful self. Poised and elegant best described her. He tapped her a little on her shoulder. She swung around and the force of her movement threw her straight into his waiting arms. He hugged her tightly, using his right hand to smoothen her hair while the left held her possessively. They were there for what seemed like eternity before she heaved herself off him to look at his face.

'Dad,' she called softly, 'Will mom be fine?' She gazed into his cute, huge eyes that now had bags of stress and sleepless nights under them.

'I believe so,' he replied. 'The doctors said so.' He rubbed his jaw endlessly, a mannerism he took up when in a pensive mood.

'I'm sorry I couldn't come to pick you from the airport,' he began to apologise.

'It's all right. I didn't encounter any difficulty coming by myself,' she assured him.

'A taxi brought you here?' he asked, looking around to see if there was any taxi parked nearby.

'No, Martins' uncle came for him so they dropped me off,' she explained.

'Martins came home with you?' he asked, not knowing why he suddenly had this knot in his throat.

'Yes, why? Oh no, Dad, not like that. He belongs to Jina and I knew it right from the start,' she said. 'Everything I did was to make mom happy and keep her out of trouble. But it didn't work, so why try more.' She shrugged her young shoulders.

'I'm so proud of you, Abbie,' he breathed.

It was a mere whisper but she heard him. 'Abbie?' she queried with eyebrows raised.

'Yes . . . I adopted the name while you were away,' he lied. 'It means "father's delight."' He smiled to hide his embarrassment at almost being caught.

'Hm . . . nice name,' she cooed. 'I like it.'

She smiled broadly as she hugged her father once more.

'So, where is your bag or didn't you come with any?' he asked.

'Oh, they are in Mr. Marc's car. I insisted they dropped me off at the hospital so they opted to take my baggage to the house for me,' she explained.

'How nice and thoughtful of them,' he responded. 'Let's get you something to eat before we go in to see your mom,' he offered.

'I would have said no, but you could do with the food and fresh air,' she observed.

She tucked her hand into the crook of his arm as they strolled down to the cafeteria for something to eat.

****

Jina heard voices outside and peered out through the window but couldn't believe her eyes. There was her Martins helping to carry luggage into the main house, luggage that belonged to Alfreda, from the look of them! What was the meaning of this? Had they been dating while he was feeding her lies? Her heart sank at the thought of it. She clutched her chest in an attempt to steady her racing heartbeat. Should she go out to greet him? No, she's too valuable, so she shouldn't sell herself that cheap. If he wasn't man enough to tell her the truth about who his heart beats for, then he was not worth fighting for. Yes, he was not worth fighting for, she concluded.

In her fury she knocked down the glass cup she was drinking from before she heard the voices outside. The crash of the glass attracted the attention of the people outside. With a few long strides, Martins stood knocking at the door.

She opened the door and stepped aside for him to gain entrance into the apartment. He walked in, shut the door behind him with his left heel, while opening his arms wide for a hug. When she didn't shift from where she stood, he raised his eyebrow for an explanation.

The lump in her throat was too large to be swallowed. Tears filled her shiny eyes and her lower lip trembled as she got angry at herself for being so soft and fragile.

'My heritage,' Martins whispered in that lovely husky voice of his, 'this is me—Martins.' He emphasised by touching his chest lightly.

Yet Jina didn't move, couldn't move. She stood rooted to the spot as tears of anguish flowed freely down her cheeks.

'Please don't cry,' Martins begged. And with one stride and another swift move of his arm, he encircled her within his embrace. 'Please, please don't cry,' he pleaded some more.

Instead of making her sobbing stop, his pleas aggravated her pain. They were so real and genuine, so loving and gentle that she wondered how a man could be this affectionate and at the same time deceptive.

'My heritage, please whatever it is that's making you cry, put it behind you. I'm here now,' he cooed into her hair, eliciting more sniffing from her.

Gradually, she quietened down and made an attempt to free herself from his warm embrace. But she couldn't, for he locked the grid with his fingers behind her back. So she looked up into his face, their eyes locked, and all she could mutter was, 'why?'

'Why what?' he asked her, confused.

He couldn't even answer the why question—why was he deceiving her when he truly loved Alfreda, or why didn't he inform her that he was coming with Alfreda? Either way, she realised she didn't need answers to those questions for they would only hurt her the more. She merely shrugged her shoulders as much as the space between them permitted and made further attempts to free herself.

But he didn't bulge. 'Ain't you happy to see me?' he asked her, searching her face.

She shut her eyes tight so the look in them wouldn't betray her. 'Answer me, please,' he pleaded in a husky voice that seems to turn her knees to jelly. She was too numbed with emotions to speak and he was too persistent and insistent on getting an answer from her.

'I missed you, Jina, so very much! Please speak to me,' he begged further.

She wanted to tell him to stop torturing her, but her voice seems to have gone on sabbatical leave.

She winced each time he spoke in such an emotion-laden voice, yet she couldn't make him stop.

The slight tap on the door by his uncle was a great relief to her, but an irritation and interruption to Martins. They straightened up and she greeted Uncle Marc warmly, though her cheek burned with embarrassment. After exchanging pleasantries, he suggested to Martins that it was about time they left for home. Martins nodded and asked to be given a couple of minutes to tidy things up with Jina. Uncle Marc obliged and stepped out after bidding Jina farewell.

'Babes, you haven't said as much as a word to me,' Martins said, looking straight into her eyes.

'What's there to say?' Jina asked, surprising both of them.

'What do you mean?' Martins asked, putting his two hands into his trouser pockets in an attempt to stop them from quivering.

'You should have told me it's Alfreda you prefer all these years,' she spat out before she could stop herself.

'Alfreda? Prefer? I . . . I don't get it, Jina,' Martins stammered, shocked at Jina's words.

'Yes, you live millions of miles away with her, you flew back to the country with her without even mentioning it to me and we have been in communication all this while,' she poured out in one breath.

'Is that what this attitude is all about?' he asked, gesturing between the two of them.

'I don't want to struggle for a man with another girl, let alone my sister,' she said and realised too late what she had just said.

'Your sister?' Martins asked with his left eyebrow raised.

'Figuratively,' she lied, feeling so rotten with herself because she had never lied to him before.

'Well, do you need my explanation or have you already drawn your conclusions?' He asked so calmly that she felt stupid starting a fight with him at this time.

'It's okay,' she said.

'The explanation or it's okay because you've drawn your conclusions?' he asked with eyes not leaving her face for a second.

'Hmmm . . . I don't know. I just . . . em . . . I really do not know what to say, but. . .'

She was interrupted by Martins' most touching words yet. 'My heritage,' he called softly, 'you can make me the happiest man on earth by marrying me or crush my whole life with just one more negative word.'

Jina wanted to say something but had no idea what to say.

'Say something,' he pleaded.

She shut her eyes and muttered. 'I don't know what to say.'

The room went dead silent. The click of the door caused Jina to open her eyes, and when she did, she discovered she was alone in the apartment. Martins had quietly slipped away leaving her with a myriad of unanswered questions.

****

'I'm sorry,' Jina said, 'I shouldn't have called you.' She spoke quietly.

Martins didn't say anything but still held the line. 'I have to go now,' Jina said.

Still Martins said nothing. After a few seconds, she dropped the call and held her head in her hands.

'Why are we like this?' she asked herself. 'It's love today, hate tomorrow; anger this minute and calm the next minute. What is the matter with us?'

****

Martins removed the receiver from his ear at the click sound signalling the end of the call and looked at it closely, as if Jina's face was etched on it, before replacing it to its original position.

'Uncle Marc,' Martins called as they drove to the hospital to see Mrs. Wilson. She was now fully awake and had requested to see Irene and Martins first, then Jina and Martins later. No one could explain why she made such requests, but they had decided to oblige her. Irene would arrive from her workplace and meet with her brother and uncle at the hospital. Jina and her mother would come later on.

'Yes?' Marc replied, glancing at his nephew briefly before focusing back on the road.

'Why don't love and common sense go hand in hand?' Martins asked.

'My dear, love is more than a feeling. It is more than an emotional package of wants and desires. Love is life, it's full of action. Anyone in love has a major role to play to keep the love nourished and strong,' Uncle Marc lectured. 'As for common sense, it judges and perceives things in a way that most people think reasonable. But love doesn't work that way; when you apply common sense to love, you will destroy love's unique qualities. Love acts, flows and nourishes, but common sense hesitates . . . that's the difference, my boy.' He ended his lecture with a little smile playing at the corners of his lips.

'Yes, Uncle, and love comes with pain . . . but she's worth the pain,' Martins muttered more to himself than to his uncle.

'You're right,' his uncle said softly, glancing at Martins intermittently as he drove. 'Love is patient, too. You've waited all these years, I guess a little while longer won't be too much to ask for.'

'Uncle, I will wait for her until she is ready. I love her, but the secrets she's keeping from me are way too much,' Martins opined.

'Women are like that,' Marc said, concentrating on the road.

'I was so pissed when I heard she worked for my late dad's lawyer, and she never mentioned it,' Martins poured out.

'Maybe she didn't know Elvis was your late dad's lawyer,' Marc defended.

'Uncle, you heard the security man. Elvis gave Jina an envelope the night he was murdered and I assume she has gone through the contents of that envelope,' Martins fumed.

'And what do you think might be the contents?' Marc asked Martins, smiling. He was trying so hard to make light of the matter. He liked Jina and would be so happy to see his nephew walk down the aisle with her to sign the dotted lines, and for them to pledge their love to each other for all times.

'Uncle Marc, you amaze me,' Martins said, hitting his uncle lightly on the shoulder.

'Amazement is better than annoyance,' Marc replied and they both laughed.

'You said Jina has secrets she is keeping from you, aside the envelope and its contents, what more is she keeping from you?' Marc asked as they drove into the hospital premises.

'Didn't know you heard that,' Martins laughed.

His uncle looked at him and just shook his head , joining him in the laughter.

****

The room where Mrs. Wilson lay suddenly became smaller with the number of people in it. Mr. Alfred Wilson stood by the window while Alfreda sat by her mother. Irene, Martins and Uncle Marc stood at the other side of the room facing Mrs. Wilson, who was getting too exhausted from talking.

'Please find a place in your hearts to forgive me. I was too desperate. I wanted to hurt your dad back, but in doing that I hurt myself and many others who did nothing to me,' she begged weakly. 'I paid the hired killers with the money I collected from your father. I told him to pay me well so I can back off and allow him enjoy his family. He did because he didn't want trouble and he loved his family so much. But I didn't back off, I planned his death and paid his killers with his money. I was so evil and wicked, please forgive me.'

Tears streamed down Irene's face at the thought of how their parents were murdered in cold blood. Martins drew her to himself, while shutting his eyes to erase the same memories. Just then, there was a slight rap on the door and Jina and her mother stepped into the already crowded room.

Martins was grateful for this beautiful interruption, because the beauty that just stepped into the room with her mother momentarily took his attention away from the confessions of the sick and dying woman. His eyes were wide and fixed on Jina but she tactfully avoided them. She smiled shyly as she greeted the other occupants of the small room. She hugged Alfreda and the teary Irene, while curtseying as she greeted Mr. Alfred Wilson and Uncle Marc. Finally, she cast him a shy glance and mouthed 'good evening, Martins.' He couldn't answer because of the lump that suddenly appeared in his throat. He nodded and smiled back at her.

'Jina, please come. . .' Mrs. Wilson called out weakly to her.

She looked at her mother, who gave her a slight nod, indicating she should go, before she stepped forward towards Mrs. Wilson's frail body on the bed.

'Will you ever forgive me?' the woman asked, trying to touch her. She was too weak to move her hand to where Jina stood.

Jina closed her eyes momentarily as she fought back the tears threatening to spill. She moved closer to the woman in bed, held her hands and allowed the tears spill and fall on their joined hands. Martins tried holding himself, but couldn't. He made his way to Jina's side and held her shoulders as she sobbed.

'Thank you, Martins, and now please take good care of her, love her, protect her, fight for her . . . you are meant for each other,' Mrs. Wilson said more faintly.

There was a sigh of relief from nearly everyone in the room as Jina fell into Martins' arms and sobbed uncontrollably. Martins patted her shoulders, reassuring her that all was well. When she had relieved herself of the bottled up emotions, she wiped her face with her two hands, turned to face Mrs. Wilson and said, 'I forgive you, Ma. I did that a very long time ago, though some recent discoveries almost brought back the hatred. But I am different now, I can no longer hate or intentionally hurt people.'

She turned to face Martins, 'Please forgive me for all the secrets I kept from you. I didn't know how you would react or handle them.' She blinked away the tears forming in her eyes.

'I might as well get everything off my chest now,' she muttered and exhaled loudly as Martins took her hand in support. She shut her eyes and braced herself to make further revelations.

'I forgive you, Mom,' she started, 'for keeping our identity a secret to us all. I found out, but couldn't open up about it to anybody except the Holy Spirit,' Jina said as she opened her eyes looked at her mother and shut them tight again.

Her mother looked at Mr. Alfred Wilson. He in turn shrugged, indicating he was unaware of what she was talking about.

'I forgive you, Mr. Wilson . . . Dad. It's very difficult and hurting to come to terms with the fact that you have been my biological father all these years without my knowledge.'

Feet shuffled and heads turned in all directions as her words poured.

'I heard the conversation between you and Mrs. Wilson here,' she said, nodding towards the bed where Mrs. Wilson lay. 'You told her I am your child just like Alfreda is. I almost choked with pain that day, but the Holy Spirit helped me get through those awful moments. Alfreda, we've been sisters all along.' She sniffed and opened her eyes to see Alfreda wiping tears from her own eyes.

'Jina,' her mother interrupted, 'it's a time of revelation and apologies and we might as well get them all over with. Alfreda is not just your sister, both of you are twins.'

Mrs. Jordan wiped her eyes with her handkerchief. Jina's eyes grew wide in astonishment and Alfreda let out a loud sob. Irene moved to hold Alfreda as Martins drew Jina to himself and held her firmly. Mr. Alfred Wilson dipped his two hands in his trouser pockets and turned to face the wall as tears of shame and pain flowed freely from his eyes.

Uncle Marc was too shocked to say anything. He shifted backwards, leaned on the wall behind him and shut his eyes tight. Sniffs and silent tears filled the hospital room. They were in this situation for a while until finally Jina cleared her throat to get everyone's attention. She gently tore herself from Martins' hold.

'Sitting here and crying over these secrets and revelations won't do us any good. The Bible says, *"in all these things we are more than conquerors."* It's also written that everything works together for our good so we should give God praise in all situations.'

She sniffed, rubbed her hands together and continued. 'I want us all to please forgive each other. The size of the hurt or pain is irrelevant before God. We should also go to God in prayer and ask Him to forgive, cleanse and strengthen us in this trying period so we won't derail in our thinking and actions. Is anyone ready to pray with me?' she asked, looking around.

'Yes,' Alfreda said, standing up.

'Yes,' Mrs. Wilson replied weakly.

The *yesses* sounded from all corners of the room.

Jina sang for a while. 'Please, before we continue, it will be good if we make peace with God first. The Bible says that the prayer of a sinner is an abomination unto the Lord. If there is any among us who hasn't made it right with God, I want such a person or persons to say a simple prayer with me and mean it in their hearts.

'Romans 10:9-10 says, "*That if thou shalt confess with thy mouth the Lord Jesus, and shalt believe in thine heart that God hath raised him from the dead, thou shalt be saved. For with the heart man believeth unto righteousness; and with the mouth confession is made unto salvation.*"

'Let's pray:

'Dear Lord God, I come to you in the Name of Jesus. I believe that Jesus Christ is the Son of the living God. I believe that You, Oh Lord, raised Him from the dead and I confess with my mouth His Lordship over my life from today. I receive by faith the remission of my sins and salvation from all manner of destruction. I have eternal life in my spirit right now; I am born again! Thank you, Lord, for making me Your dwelling place, in Jesus' Name, Amen.'

Mr. Wilson, Mrs. Wilson, Alfreda and Uncle Marc were those who said the prayers. Jina prayed for them and the presence of God filled the little room—it was quite tangible! None could deny or ignore God's presence in that room. When Martins described it later, he likened it to the experience the disciples of Jesus had in the upper room in Bible days.

Mrs. Wilson kept muttering, 'Thank you, Lord, I have eternal life now. I have eternal life in my spirit.' She was excited in her spirit.

After the prayers, Jina gave them brief exhortation on what eternal life was and what it entailed.

'It is the life of God. It's not the life you will live when you get to heaven, it is the gift of God to us now in this world! This life is indestructible, stronger than sickness and diseases. Eternal life is the life that makes God, God! The Greek call it

Zoe. It's the essence of Christianity. It's the divine life working in the human body. I am so glad that we are all partakers of this life by virtue of our accepting Jesus Christ as our Lord and Saviour. There is nothing to worry about anymore. . .'

As she was speaking, there was a slight cough from Mrs. Wilson. All attention shifted towards her. She had begun breathing faster than usual. Uncle Marc and Mr. Wilson rushed out to call the doctor and nurses. The others drew closer to her, praying, speaking and doing all sorts. But before the medical team arrived, Mrs. Wilson breathed her last. With a small smile playing at the corners of her mouth, she gave up the ghost.

The medical team rushed in and solemnly confirmed her dead. There was pin drop silence in the room as the different faces there looked at each other with many questions running through their minds.

'But she wasn't looking that bad,' Martins spoke up first.

'Looking is different from feeling,' the doctor replied.

'She may have been enduring the pains in order not to upset you all,' a nurse chipped in.

They were thrown into that pensive mood again, with no one speaking except for the medical team writing their report and making arrangements to move her body to the mortuary.

Mr. Alfred Wilson was dazed. Though they had not been best of friends in the recent times, her death few minutes after giving her life to Christ and making peace with everyone around her was quite a drama.

Alfreda stood up from where she had sat numbly and walked to her father. She reached out, hugged him tight and placed her head on his shoulders, shutting her eyes tight. Tears flowed freely from her eyes. Jina left Martins' side and went to her twin sister and father. They included her in the embrace as each spoke softly to comfort the other.

All procedures done and over with, Mrs. Wilson's body was wheeled to the mortuary while Mrs. Jordan packed the late woman's personal items into a bag. Mr. Wilson and Uncle Marc left for the hospital's administrative block to pay the hospital bill and the rest headed to the car park.

Intuitively, Jina and Alfreda took each other's hand and walked silently ahead of the troupe, while Martins and Irene walked behind them. Martins took one more look at the joined hands of the young women in front of him and became angry. 'How can these ladies be twins all along and this knowledge was hidden from them? How can one be that callous?' he mused within himself.

As he was boiling inside, his sister took a hold of his balled fist and whispered tenderly to his hearing alone, 'don't fix your gaze on things that drain you, fix your mind on your strength and see yourself soar higher and higher.'

He looked at her and smiled warmly. He didn't understand how she read his mind so easily. He gave her hand a loving squeeze and she smiled back at him. They headed to the car park silently, yet with volumes said.

****

'Jina, please reconsider your stand,' Mrs. Jordan pleaded with her daughter again. 'He is your father. All he wants is for us to unite as one family that we originally were. Don't keep pushing him away, please.'

'Mom, you once taught me to always stand my ground and not allow swaying and changing circumstances to change me and I think I am just applying that now,' Jina replied, still folding her clothes and putting them in a travelling bag.

'Jina, this case is different. Your father wants to be part of our lives henceforth,' Mrs. Jordan continued, sniffing harder.

'"Don't run into relationship because of what you need, go into them because of what you have to offer." Mom, do you remember this statement?' Jina asked her mom. 'This relationship you want us to go into now, what do we have to offer the people concerned?' She had momentarily stopped what she was doing to fix her gaze on her mother, who looked down and wondered what answer to give her daughter.

Since the death and burial of Mrs. Wilson, Jina had been moody and unresponsive to everybody. Martins had finally left her alone after her erratic behaviour towards him. The only person she managed to relate well with was her twin sister, Alfreda. Martins had long returned to Canada to conclude his final thesis and pick up his certificate. He had pleaded with Jina to marry him, but she had refused. Her reason? She was yet to find out if what they felt for each other was genuine or not.

'Imagine!' Her mother shuddered at those words when Martins recounted them to her before leaving. Alfreda hinted that Jina had asked *her* if she loved Martins enough to marry him. When Alfreda responded in the negative, Jina said she would wait for Alfreda to get married first before she would accept a proposal from any man.

'Why?' Mrs. Jordan asked her second daughter.

'I don't know. I find her words and action strange sometimes,' Alfreda replied with concern in her voice.

'Well, Jina,' Mrs. Jordan started, focusing again on her Jina, 'since you don't want to reconsider your stand on this matter, I am going over to the main house. We are all having dinner there. Join us if you want to,' she finished and left their apartment briskly.

Jina sat down on her bed, pushed the clothes she was folding to one side and buried her face in her hands.

'What's the matter with me?' she asked herself, 'Why am I angry at everybody?'

As a kid, she had fantasized about a lovely, beautiful family. She had daydreamed about them having lunch and dinner together, laughing and making small talk over things. Now, her daydream was thrust on her in reality and she didn't want to accept it.

167

Thinking through all of these, it dawned on her that so much had happened in the last few months: the discoveries of who her true parents were and about her twin sister, who had been nasty to her all those years at the instigation of her adoptive mother. Not forgetting, the death of her boss, the wonders of her little sermon, which had delivered salvation to her real father, twin sister and Mrs. Wilson. The marriage proposal from Martins was just another case and she still didn't know if he loved her or her twin sister! Lastly, the great family reunion that had been beckoning on her. Phew! They were too many, she needed some time to digest all of these and take a clear decision as to what she wanted.

She quickly finished packing her bag and zipped it up after throwing in some toiletries. She took one more glance at their apartment, checked the envelope she dropped on the table to ensure it contained the right information. She exhaled loudly, opened the door quietly and made her exit.

She saw Old Soldier sitting outside his security post. This was not what she had bargained for. What explanation would she give him now to let her off the hook? She inhaled and exhaled deeply and walked on with a straight face. 'Old Soldier, good evening, sir,' she greeted without stopping.

'Good evening, my daughter. May the Lord guide you safely to your destination,' he prayed. 'Amen,' she responded and quickly exited the compound to enter the taxi waiting for her.

She truly needed a break from everything. Thank heavens Julia had chosen this time to invite her to Ghana. She'd wanted to say no but looking at the whole scenario now, she was glad she hadn't. Her mother would feel bad and hurt, Martins would be disappointed, but she needed to do this for herself—and all of them. Maybe, when she gets back, or better put, *if* she gets back she would be in a better frame of mind, she would reason better and handle issues better.

'Yes, Jesus occasionally withdrew from His disciples and the multitude to a quiet place to commune with the Father,' the Voice within her said.

She nearly jumped out of her skin. It had been a while since she heard Him speak; she had almost forgotten His existence.

'Really?' She smiled when she got her breath back. 'Okay, so I'm not making a mistake! I was almost knocking myself on the head for doing this,' she poured out to Him.

'The steps of the righteous are ordered by the Lord,' the Voice reminded her.

'Thank you, Lord,' she breathed as she heaved herself into the back seat of the taxi.

'Good evening, sir,' she greeted the taxi driver. 'I'm sorry I kept you waiting,' she apologised.

'It's OK, ma. I didn't wait for too long,' the driver replied. They kept the conversation minimal as they drove to the airport.

As she made to switch off her phone in preparation to board her flight, she saw her mother's call. Should she pick it or ignore it? Ignoring it would be rude and she wasn't known for rudeness, so she picked it.

'Hello, Mom,' she answered, closing her eyes, knowing what would follow.

'Jina Jordan, where are you?' her mother queried at the other end of the line.

'I am very safe where I am, Mom,' she replied calmly.

'That's not the answer to my question,' her mother shot back.

'Mom, I am very fine and I have to go now. I will talk to you later, Mom, bye,' she said and cut the call before her mother could say any other thing.

She boarded the flight to Accra, Ghana, and heaved a sigh of relief.

Was she running away from challenges and realities? No, she was not. She wanted people to see things from her perspective, she wanted people to believe what she believed, and to win this battle she needed to go and recharge herself and show up again at the battle front.

She smiled at her analogy and rested her head on her headrest. She shut her eyes as the plane taxied and finally made its ascent into the deep blue sky.

****

'Hope you enjoyed the programme,' Julia said to Jina, smiling as they made their way out of the over-crowded hall where they have been for the past four hours.

'It wasn't bad,' Jina replied, smiling back at her friend.

'It's a quarter past six p.m., you want us to go home or to go take some fresh air somewhere? It's a little too early to head home now, if you ask me,' Julia said.

'You are my hostess so I will follow your leading,' Jina replied, still smiling.

'In that case, let's go catch some more fun elsewhere,' Julia said as she unlocked her car door and Jina slipped into the front seat. They both threw their handbags onto the back seat, looked at each other and laughed at their simultaneous action.

The place Julia drove to was a recreational park, beautifully decorated and well-lit as it was almost dusk. The sight of the waterfalls was breathtaking and Jina couldn't hide her excitement as she beamed with smiles.

'I love this place,' she squeaked.

'I'm glad you love it,' Julia replied, giving her friend a bear hug.

They strolled hand in hand towards the coffee shop. Jina's admiration for that environment was palpable. They ordered coffee and argued about who would pay the bill. Eventually Julia won. She was the hostess, she claimed.

As she made to give the money to the coffee attendant, a baritone voice spoke softly behind them, jolting them in the process.

'I will pay for the coffee, ladies, that's if you don't mind,' he said.

Julia turned around and beheld the most handsome face she had ever seen. She tried to smile, but the smile froze as she saw the shock on her friend's face. Jina was almost white with shock as she gazed at the intruder with her mouth slightly open.

'Surprised, my Heritage?' the young man asked with his gaze fixed on Jina.

'You know her, young man?' Julia asked in defence of her guest.

'Yes, she is my . . .'

'What are you doing here?' Jina asked, cutting him short.

'I was about asking you same question. But because I'm a gentleman, I will answer you and you will answer mine too,' he breathed.

Jina rolled her eyes and gave a slight nod, indicating she was in.

'Okay, I'm done with my programme in Canada. I was heading home when a friend of mine invited me to his only sister's wedding. The wedding took place yesterday. I should've been on my way today, but I had this very strong pull to stick around for a few more days. Now, I know what the pull was all about,' he explained, smiling mischievously.

Jina couldn't help but smile too at his sweetness and his amazing way of handling things.

'Before I answer you, meet Julia, my friend. We were course mates in Law School and did our court attachment in the same court,' Jina explained.

'Nice meeting you, Julia,' he said, offering her a quick handshake.

'And, Julia. . .' Jina began, then stopped to clear her throat of a lump that had just found its way there. 'Julia, meet Martins, the one and only Martins you've heard of since we met.'

She then burst into laughter as Julia squeaked and jumped onto Martins' shoulder before he had the chance to steady himself. Both of them staggered, but didn't fall. Martins was fast on his feet and had managed to steady himself.

He looked at Jina with adoration, a bemused smile playing around his lips. 'What an introduction!' he managed to say.

'It's an honour to meet my friend's heartthrob in my own country,' Julia exclaimed.' I was hosting a friend but now I'm hosting a couple!' she reeled out joyously.

The coffee attendant cleared his throat and they realised they were still owing him. Martins paid up while the ladies carried their coffee and stepped out of the shop.

Martins looked at Jina for an explanation but got a wink instead. His heart pounded in his chest. Did it mean she had accepted his proposal? If yes, why hadn't she called him all this while, and what in the world was she doing in Ghana—so far away from home?

Another young man strolled towards them carrying two snack bags.

'Hi everyone,' he greeted and looked at Martins for an explanation.

'Ladies, meet Kwame, my close friend. Kwame, meet Jina and her friend, Julia,' he said casually, not wanting to offend Jina, for he is enjoying *this* new Jina.

'Jina?' Kwame asked. 'The same Jina or another one?' He looked confused.

'The one and same Jina,' Martins replied, nodding his head for emphasis.

'Wow, this is good!' Kwame exclaimed. 'Excited meeting you, ladies,' he said, raising his elbow for a handshake as his hands were full with the bags of snacks.

The evening stood still for them as Martins and Jina had a lot of catching up to do. It was a few minutes to ten p.m. when they reluctantly called it a day with a promise to see each other the next day. The young men escorted the ladies to their car and waited for them to drive off before heading to where Kwame's car was parked.

'What a day!' Kwame said, heaving himself into the driver's seat.

'What a surprise would be a better statement,' Martins replied, running his fingers through his hair.

'My friend is in love lalala . . . la,' Kwame sang playfully as he raced the car out of the parking lot.

****

Jina couldn't sleep that night. Who would have thought she would run into Martins in Ghana!

The same Martins that made her leave home in the first place! She came to Ghana to think straight. Well, what an amazing way to be thinking straight, she mused.

'The footsteps of the righteous are ordered by the Lord,' the Voice within her said.

'Lord, did you plan this?' she asked childishly.

'Go to Jeremiah, chapter one verse five,' the Voice said.

Jina quickly took her cell phone and scrolled to the Bible App she had installed that afternoon with Julia's help. The App had several offline Bible versions but she fell in love with The Message Translation the instant it was installed. She hurriedly scrolled to Jeremiah 1:5 and read thus, *'Before I shaped you in the womb, I knew all about you. Before you saw the light of day, I had holy plans for you. . .'*

Jina fell on her knees and began praying to the awesome, amazing and Almighty God Who, though very big, still fit into her tiny heart. She wept sore in her praise and worship. She was truly filled with God's goodness and lost in His love. She prayed for direction and asked God to forgive her doubts while strengthening her faith in Him. It was an awesome moment for her and by the time she got up from her kneeling position, she realised she'd been there for three hours. But she had no regrets. She knew that her future and matters of her destiny were settled and settled for good.

She made two resolutions upon rising from her knees—One was to call Martins and apologise for being childish and myopic all this while and to thank him for his patience. The other was to call home and speak with her mom, twin sister and father if he was around.

As if in answer to her thoughts, her cell phone beeped and she picked it up to see an envelope sign indicating the arrival of a text message. She opened it and her heart flew to her mouth. She gasped in excitement as she read:

'Good morning to you, my heritage. Do I still stand a chance with you? Please will you marry me? Martins'

Tears of joy flowed down her cheeks blurring her vision, but she typed her reply:

'Yes, Yes, Yes, and Yes!!!'She pressed the send button and the message was delivered to Martins.

She wanted to call her family; but it was too early in the morning to make a call so she sent an SMS to her twin sister instead. It read:

'Hey, sis, don't be mad at me. Tell Mom and Dad to forgive me. I am good and I believe you are too. I ran into Martins here in Ghana yesterday (surprised?) and, yes, I have accepted his marriage proposal . . . I love you all. Will call later this morning. Bye, Jina.'

She tapped the send button and heaved a sigh of relief as she laid back on the bed, grateful for all that had happened and would still happen to her.

EPILOGUE

The gorgeously dressed Martins stood before the priest. His heart thumped excitedly. Jina was marching towards him on her father's arm.

It was finally here, the day he had dreamt of as a kid, the day she became *his* officially, the day the name he called her would really be who she was. She'd always been his heritage. He believed that God sent her his way to restore him back to God. She came as an answer to the prayer of many but specifically as the illumination to light up his dark heart, yes, as warmth to his cold soul. A wry smile twitched the corners of his mouth and he exhaled loudly. This was the day the Lord had made and truly he would rejoice and be glad in it.

Jina felt her hand being squeezed softly by her dad, who had been beaming with smiles all morning. Alfreda was her maid of honour and Julia was part of her long bridal train. She came all the way from Ghana to be a part of the grand occasion. She was truly a friend, Jina mused, remembering it was at Julia's insistence that she made that trip to Ghana, the trip she was now so grateful for.

She looked up and her gaze met Martins' and locked. Her throat tightened up with excitement and her lips parted in a king-size smile. Her smile melted his heart and he gave her a generous wink and exhaled loudly again.

He thought about the toast on their wedding invitation card. He remembered how both of them had independently come up with the same statement—word for word. His mind ran over those words again as Jina finally got to the podium where he stood with Kwame, who was his bestman, and he realised once more that he had made the right choice:

Yes, the Lines Are Fallen Unto Me
In Pleasant Places
And Yea, I have a **Goodly Heritage***!*
(Psalms 16:6)

The End!

ABOUT THE AUTHOR

Agu, Jaachynma N.E. is a successful, dynamic, prolific and best-selling author. She is a graduate of Languages and Linguistics Department of the prestigious University of Jos, Nigeria; a Chief Administrative Officer with a Federal Government Establishment; a loving wife and a caring mother; a teacher, a mentor and an advocate of women empowerment.

The Executive Director of the KingsTreasureHouse Concept, a highly respected role model, and an inspiration to many, she shares motivational insights with her generation and those yet to be born via her write ups, books, et al.

She lives in Nigeria with her beloved family comprising of her heartthrob, Dr. Aham and their two gorgeous heritages from the Lord: KING and EDWALD.

ABOUT THE BOOK

Martins' parents died when he needs them most, their death took a part of him that housed feelings and emotions. As a result, he became hard like a diamond and cold like an ice.

Jina comes from a poor family background, asthmatic and allergic to cold regions. With no money for proper medical treatment, she resorts to divine treatment.

Martins and Jina are classmates, competitors for the highest mark; instead of this making them mad against each other, it made them friends. Martins travels abroad to further his studies, in his absence, a plot against him and Jina is hatched by people supposedly stronger than them. They are forced to part ways, Jina meets a Friend, Comforter, Instructor, Teacher all rolled into one! She establishes her faith in this Friend. She gets rooted and grounded in His Word and Love. Her desires and dreams centre on this her new found Love!

Martins comes home after his studies, things happen a little too fast; their main opposition: Mrs. Wilson dies and they were free to love again. He asked for Jina's hand in marriage but will she accept? She needn't abandon her new found Love- they can all fuse into the union, they can all inherit each other and emerge as one another's HERITAGE!

www.ingramcontent.com/pod-product-compliance
Lightning Source LLC
Chambersburg PA
CBHW031454260626
47154CB00017B/2708